Preaching Lies

A novel by:

Denora M. Boone

Copyright © 2017 Denora M. Boone
Published by Anointed Inspirations Publishing

Note: This is a work of fiction. Names, characters, places and incidents either are products of the author's imagination or are used fictitiously. Any resemblance to actual events or locales or persons, living or dead, is entirely coincidental

Anointed Inspirations Publishing is currently accepting Urban Christian Fiction, Inspirational Romance, and Young Adult fiction submissions. For consideration please send manuscripts to
info@anointedinspirationspublishing.com

Connect with Denora socially
Facebook: www.facebook.com/AuthorDenora
Twitter: www.twitter.com/mzboone27
Instagram: @mzboone81
www.authordenora.com

God.

My Husband Byron.

Our children (Jalen, Elijah, Mekiyah, and Isaiah).

#AIP.

My readers.

These are the ones I do this for and the ones who won't allow me to quit. For that, all of my thanks go to them!

Love,

Dee

~1~

"Then thou shalt cut off her hand, thine eye shall not pity her." Deuteronomy 25:12

December 24, 1999

"Will you be gone long?" Kenya asked looking up from the beautiful face of her two week old daughter. She was still bedridden after the emergency C-section that she had to have so she was hoping that her fiancé would stick around long enough for her to get some rest. The medicine that she was taking for the pain was finally beginning to take effect and she just wanted to sleep.

"Nah. I just gotta make this run right quick and I'll be back," Keys told her without making eye contact. He did that whenever he was lying and Kenya picked up on it immediately.

"But it's Christmas Eve Keys and our daughter's first Christmas!"

Sucking her teeth, she turned her attention back to their daughter who was feasting on her left breast. Kenya couldn't wait until she could move around and make bottles on the regular because as soon as she could it was a wrap on breast feeding. She didn't care anything about it being one of the ways that she could lose her pregnancy weight or that it was a healthier option for her baby. Her little princess was draining her and she was over it.

"Why is it that every time I leave the house you gotta cause a problem?" Keys asked this time with his handsome face balled up.

Kenya hated when he looked at her that way. His 6'3 frame which was covered in tattoos was already intimidating enough to her but it was something about his eyes. She wouldn't call them hazel but they weren't quite green. Maybe gold. They resembled the eyes of a tiger that was stalking his prey. Her grandmother down south would say that he had "those funny colored eyes" and Kenya would have to agree. They were beautiful when he was in a good mood but when Keys wasn't, which was most of the time, they seemed to penetrate her soul and not in a good way.

She didn't know why she even bothered asking him when he was coming back because she knew that it was a sure way to start a fight, but she prayed that this time would be different. Their baby girl had now entered the world and the whole time she was pregnant he promised her that he would slow down once she arrived. Well for the last fourteen days things around their small Bronx apartment were the same as it had been before she gave birth.

Letting out a frustrated breath, Kenya put the baby down on her stomach now that she was fast asleep. The caramel face held freckles that were identical to her mother's including a deep set of dimples but behind her closed eyelids were the eyes of her father. Kenya hoped that was the only thing that she had inherited of his because she didn't know just how she would be able to put up with two people that had the same temper.

"You breathing hard Ken. Something you need to get off your chest?"

Keys watched her intently as she turned her back to him slowly and tried her best not to aggravate the incision on her lower stomach or wake his sleeping princess. Believe it or not Keys wanted to be home with his girl and their daughter but the streets called. It was the streets that afforded them the lifestyle that they were living even if it was the day before Christmas. The fruits of his street labor were the reason that the Christmas tree was almost hidden by the many gifts that surrounded it.

When Keys met Kenya she knew what he was into and the life he lived but when she got pregnant it was as if her thought process changed. He didn't expect her to understand where he was coming from as a man so he dealt with the attitude she gave off. Yeah he had made her a promise to leave all of that behind but the money was too good and he had promised his father that he would never be a bum or a dead beat.

"Lock the door on your way out," Kenya told him as she flipped through the channels on the muted television.

"I'll be back."

"Mmm hmm."

Not one to beg any woman or apologize for anything, Keys placed his two guns in the back of his jeans and walked down the hall. Making sure the door was locked he jogged down the five flights of steps before making it outside and jumping in his brand new all white Mercedes Benz SL. It was twenty six degrees out and the sky looked like it was about to drop some mean snowflakes. That cancelled his plans of pushing his whip with the top down. He would just have to stunt another time. Keys started the car and before he pulled off he put the issue with his woman to the back of his mind and focused on staying aware of his surroundings.

Everything that Keys did caused the next man to hate and that afforded him plenty of enemies. He made sure to keep his ears to the streets and stay three steps ahead of the competition and the police. In all the years that he had been contributing to the drug habits of fiends that littered the streets he had it on lock. From New York all the way down to the DMV, Keys had never been caught slipping so that day would be no different. Or so he thought.

***

Kenya felt like she had been asleep for hours but in reality it was only a short while before she heard what sounded like the door being knocked off its hinges. She jumped up as fast as her aching body could and listened intently.

"Maybe I was dreaming," she said softly to herself before she heard something fall in the front room.

Her adrenaline was now pumping and no pain could be felt. Only the need for survival and if not her own at least her daughter's. Quickly she picked up her sleeping daughter and kissed her face before saying a quick prayer.

"God I know I'm not in any position to really ask for anything because I left you long ago but please watch

over my baby girl. Don't let her get hurt and give her the life that she deserves. Forgive me God."

Just as she placed the baby in the bottom drawer of her dresser and grabbed her own gun from the top, the door to her room burst open.

POW! POW! POW!

"Ahhhh!" Kenya screamed out in pain before returning fire of her own.

She was hit but she wasn't giving up. Kenya knew the consequences of dealing with someone like Keys. With that kind of lifestyle came the very real possibilities of them all losing their lives but she was all in.

POW! POW! POW! POW!

Thump!

If Kenya was going to die she was going to take someone with her. No need for her family to be the only one shedding tears.

Her family.

They were against her relationship with Kenya from the beginning. Flashes of her mother's disapproving face went through her mind as she continued to fire. Granny Liz was constantly praying that she would move on from Keys but her heart was bonded to his. There was no going back and honestly Kenya didn't want to. Keys was her all and she loved him more than anything.

Except their child.

Why wasn't she crying? There were too many bullets sounding off for her not to be awaken from the deep sleep she was in.

"My baby!" Kenya tried screaming but couldn't. That's when she noticed for the first time where she had been hit. Instantly her free hand went to her throat as she tried to move her body towards the dresser. She just had to make sure her only child was ok. Kenya needed her to be so that she could die in peace. Her death was inevitable.

It felt like to Kenya that she had a ton of bricks piled on her body making it hard to move and even harder when she saw blood dripping from the bottom of the dresser where her baby lay.

"Noooooo."

Blood was filling up her lungs and coming out of her mouth simultaneously causing her screams to sound muffled like she was under water. Still, knowing her time was winding down she was full of anger. Because of the decisions that both she and Keys made their daughter wouldn't live past the two weeks she had been in this world. So, before she died she was going to make sure their murderer met her in hell.

Gun still gripped as tightly as she could hold it she lifted her head towards the movement in her room. A shadow covered her the moment her vision started to go.

"Keys thought it was ok to steal from me?" the voice asked rhetorically.

Kenya knew that voice and knew it well. Satan himself stood above her with the barrel of his gun trained on her and she wearily returned the gesture with her own gun.

"Still a fighter I see."

With everything in her, Kenya spit on his shoes.

The ultimate form of disrespect.

That millisecond of losing focus because she was angry gave him just what he needed in order to release the bullet that put Kenya out of her misery.

"And still disrespectful too."

With those final words, the man stepped back and looked at the bodies around him smiling. He wasn't worried about the police showing up right away because he had most of them on his payroll. He couldn't help but to smile knowing that the woman he had always wanted by his side was just as gutter as he was. She had taken out all three of the men that he had run up in her and her man's apartment with.

Reaching behind him he pulled out his favorite machete that he carried with him and swiftly cut off the hand that held the five carat engagement ring. Bending down he picked up the dismembered hand and removed the ring. Closing her lifeless eyes for the last time he stood up and backed away. Although he knew she was no longer alive he spoke to her anyway as if she was.

"Save a seat in hell for Chop beautiful."

~2~

"Having a form of godliness but denying the power thereof; from such turn away."

2 Timothy 3:5

Pastor Reynolds ended his soul stirring sermon and sat down before the last offering began. He had preached so hard that he had to unbutton the top button of his perfectly pressed white shirt and remove his suit jacket. He graciously accepted the cold glass of ice water that his armor bearer brought to him just like he had done every Sunday.

Looking around the huge church that held close to five thousand members he smiled broadly. Never in a million years did he think that he would be standing in front of people and bringing a word to the people of God. No matter how many times his grandmother said that he was a Man of God it didn't show. He had other dreams but circumstances changed his course so there he was. A pastor. A man that people came to in order to receive healing and whatever else they needed from a higher and greater power that spoke through him.

Once the last person had come up to give unto the storehouse, one of his other ministers gave the benediction. Some members began filing out of the building while some hung around fellowshipping with one another. That was his que to make his way to the floor and greet some of the people who had either just joined or wanted to speak with him for one reason or another.

"Lord Pastor that was a powerful word you gave today! I know the angels in heaven are rejoicing and God is well pleased," one of his members rushed up to tell him.

It was the same routine for Sister Brianna every week and he was quite frankly tired of the same line. Maybe if she said something new he would believe that she meant it and wasn't just trying to get him in her bed. Bri as she insisted he call her, which he never did, was known to have 'the spirit of the woman at the well' on her life that she wasn't trying to release.

"Thank you Sister Brianna. That's very kind of you," he told her politely.

"Now Pastor what did I tell you? Call me Bri," she responded in a flirtatious manner. Swiping her hand down his arm and letting it linger a second too long.

The sound of someone clearing their throat got the attention of both of them and Brianna's smile immediately faded.

"Pastor we need you to come and sign off on the count for the deposit tomorrow," his assistant spoke with an unpleasant look on her face.

There was no secret about how the two women felt about one another and neither of them tried to hide it. They had even come to blows at one of the church picnics almost a year ago. It had taken at least three deacons to get them off of each other.

"Is there anything else you needed?" Pastor Reynolds asked Brianna.

"Well I need to talk to you in *private*," she said putting emphasis on the word 'private'.

"Make an appointment just like everyone else. Pastor is a busy man and there is no special treatment for anyone. When you call I'll see what he has available," Shaunie stated before turning her attention back to him. "Deacon Poole is ready." With that she walked off and so did he leaving Brianna standing there looking stuck.

"I'll be glad when Satan comes to get his minion so she can stay out of Pastor's face," one of the mothers stated with disgust lacing her voice.

"And I wish you would let somebody wax that mustache above your lip. Or at least let them line it up to match your goatee," Brianna snapped back.

"You disrespectful little harlot! There's a special place for people like you," Mother Allen jumped in to defend her friend.

"Shole is…right under Elder Allen," Brianna retorted referring to the woman's husband. "And tell him I want my money up front for my services next time."

Everyone within earshot stood stunned with the revelation of Brianna sleeping with the older man. It was that good hot church tea that members only gossiped about and speculated on, but to now hear it was true was a bit much. Best believe though that by the time everyone made it home from church every regular member would know about it even if they hadn't heard it for themselves. That's just how some church folks were. Loved to spread the mess but closed their hearts to the message of God.

***

"I don't know why you let her get to you," Pastor Reynolds told Shaunie the moment they got into his office and closed the door.

"Because Hosea you know she's just trying to get with you. You're the only man in this church that she hasn't sunk her acrylic nails into."

Pastor Reynolds, whose first name was Hosea, looked at the masterpiece of a woman that stood before him. Her thick frame was stacked in all of the right places while her peanut butter skin was blemish free. Shaunie had her hair cut short and rocked it in some burgundy finger waves. She had a small nose piercing in her left nostril and her eyes were adorned with a set of the longest and thickest eyelashes that he had ever seen on a woman. God had surely hand crafted her and the view was amazing.

"Now how would that look if the people of God knew their beloved pastor was smashing more than one woman in the church?" he asked with a raised brow and that panty dropping smile that drove all the women crazy. Especially Shaunie.

Shaunie sauntered over to where her lover was sitting behind his desk to give him some of what she liked to call her 'anointing', but before she could straddle his lap there was a knock at the door.

"Come in," Hosea yelled once he and Shaunie made sure that nothing was out of place or would look awkward for anyone that was on the other side of the door.

The door opened and in walked his daughter Haven causing Shaunie to roll her eyes the moment her eyes landed on the girl. For some reason, no matter how nice Shaunie tried to be to Haven, Haven couldn't stand her so the feeling was mutual. Neither she nor Hosea had let their relationship be known because he claimed he wanted to keep that from his daughter until he knew where their relationship was going. Shaunie thought it was because of his fiancé, who died when his daughter was three years old. Part of her felt like he was still holding on to a woman that wasn't coming back just because his fat daughter still hadn't gotten over not having a mother. Maybe, if she took all of that energy she used to cry about a dead woman and put it towards a workout, she wouldn't have time to worry about what her father did. She was almost grown and was going to leave home soon for college, so Hosea needed to have a life of his own. It wasn't as if he was always there like he should have been anyway because his ministry was first priority.

Shaunie couldn't lie even if she wanted to when it came to Haven's appearance. The girl was a gorgeous but she was just fat. She was one of those big girls with the pretty face type chicks but her self-esteem was horrible. She never dressed like the young girls her age. No trendy outfits or hairstyles. Instead she dressed like the old women in the church. Long skirts, ugly blouses, stockings, and kitten heels. What senior in high school wore kitten heels?

"Hey Daddy!" Haven greeted him like he was the only one in the room causing her best friend Mila to snicker.

Shaunie didn't like her little fast tail either. Haven and Mila were literally like night and day and she didn't even understand how they were so tight. Whereas Haven was the goody-two-shoes, Mila was hell-in-stilettos but for some reason everyone thought she was innocent. Shaunie knew better and that was only because they both copped their weed from the same person. She had gone to buy some one day and when she entered the trap house Mila was sitting up in there getting higher than a little bit and letting some little corner boy feel all on her. When she saw Shaunie walk in she wasn't even trying to run and hide. Mila wore an expression that let Shaunie know she was unbothered by her presence.

When Shaunie threatened to tell on her and finally let everyone know the type of girl she really was Mila burst out laughing and almost choked on the weed smoke she had just inhaled into her young lungs. Mila told her if she was to tell on her that she would also have to explain why she was even in a trap house to begin with. That would look worse on her than a rebellious teenage girl who was expected to try and buck against the parental system. From that day on Shaunie knew not to let her attitude get the best of her because that would only give Mila a reason to expose her. Shaunie had plans of marrying Hosea and nothing was going to come between her and her goal of becoming the first lady of The Blood of Jesus COGIC.

"Hey baby girl. Hey MiMi," Hosea greeted them before standing and giving the girls a hug.

"Daddy can I go to Mila's house to finish our project? It's due tomorrow and we wanted to add some stuff to it."

"Of course baby girl. Just be home before it gets too late."

"We will. Thanks Daddy."

Kissing her father Haven walked back toward the door to leave still not acknowledging Shaunie. Mila followed behind her to leave but not before she stuck her middle finger up at Shaunie. Right before Shaunie got ready to call her out about her behavior, Mila discretely placed her thumb and index finger to her lips like she was smoking a blunt shutting Shaunie right up.

She was so deep in her thoughts that she hadn't even realized Hosea had made his way to her until he wrapped his arms around her waist.

"Now where were we?" he asked seductively causing her to grin.

Immediately nothing else mattered but the time she was about to spend with her man. Locking the door she pushed him down on the couch and prepared to lay hands and anoint the man of God.

~3~

"I will fear no evil for thou art with me..." Psalms 23:4

"Still be playing with pot and pans, call me Quavo Ratatouille," Mila sang the famous line to Migos song *Bad and Boujee.* As soon as the girls heard the beat coming around the corner Mila immediately threw her hands in the air, tooted her lips up, and began dancing. She was moving her arms like she was waving flags above her head then switched it up like she was stirring something on a stove. Haven couldn't help but to laugh at her friend just as the car blasting the music came to a stop.

Haven looked around in a panic to make sure that no one from the church was coming down the street. Mila didn't live far from the church so they decided to walk once her father had given her the go ahead. The last thing she wanted was for someone to see the two of them talking to two thugs in a car that she was positive they were too young to be driving. Haven knew it cost a lot of money and for them to be driving it meant one thing. Dope boys.

"Aye slim thick in the blue dress," the boy on the passenger side called out to Mila. Haven knew he wasn't talking to her because she may have been thick but she definitely was far from slim.

"What's up Zaddy?" Mila crooned showing her new set of teeth. It had been over a month since she got her braces removed and she had been smiling ever since.

"Where y'all bout to go?" he asked her.

Mila had a thing for ugly boys and Haven couldn't understand it. It wasn't like she had room to talk or that she was hung up on looks but the boys Mila gravitated to were the ones who had faces that only their mothers could love. The boy in the front seat fit that description to a tee. He had a huge gap between his top teeth and his pale skin looked like he had never seen a Proactive infomercial a day in his life. From where Haven stood she could tell that the only thing he had going for himself was his good grade of hair which was pulled up into a man bun and he could dress his behind off. The Gucci shirt he wore gave that away but what Mila was drawn to was the ice that dripped from his ears down to his neck and rested peacefully around his wrist. She was a sucker for money and Haven assumed that was what drew her to the ugly ones with it.

"Why you standing over there looking all scared?" the driver called out to her and snapping Haven from her thoughts.

Lord that boy is beautiful, Haven thought to herself.

"Oh no reason," she replied to him. She couldn't help but to start tugging at the shirt she wore that was a little snug on her immediately becoming self-conscious of her appearance. Something she always did when she was nervous or people outside of the church looked at her.

It was as if she felt like they were calling her the names that taunted her daily. *Fat*, *sloppy*, *rotund* were all that she saw in the mirror each night as she cried no matter how many people told her how gorgeous she was. She saw something different.

Getting out of the car the driver walked around the front and stepped up to Haven. She felt like her heart was about to jump out of her chest and at any minute her legs were going to give out. He was so tall and handsome that she wanted to reach out and touch him to see if he was real.

The gorgeous stranger towered over her so much she had to look up at him. His caramel skin looked like it was kissed by the sun and not at all like his friend's. The top of his hair was curly while the sides were cut low and edged up to perfection. He was wearing a Lakers jersey that allowed his toned and tattooed arms to be seen. One tattoo in particular stood out to her the most and it was a scripture, well a partial one, Psalms 23:4. The only part that he had embedded into his skin said, *"I will fear no evil for thou art with me."*

"Where's the rest?" Haven asked him surprising even herself. She was never the one to start a conversation and with a boy at that.

Confused he asked, "The rest of what?"

"The scripture."

Looking down at his arm he understood what she meant.

"To me this was the most powerful part of the whole thing. I know God is with me so I won't fear. Everything else will fall into place," he shrugged still looking at his arm.

"What church do you go to?" Haven inquired.

"Honestly, it's been a minute. I believe in God or whatever but that's about it. I know it has to be somebody keeping me alive with the life I live. Anyway, what's your name?"

"Haven."

"Word. That's different. I like it."

"Thanks. What's your name?"

"Asa." He decided not to tell her that Trouble was his street name. The last thing he wanted her to do was start looking for information on him.

"Fitting," she replied while smiling.

There was an awkward pause between the two of them as they just stared at each other for a few seconds before Haven looked away first. He could tell that she was nervous but something about her made him interested. His eyes trailed her body and though she was a little bigger than most of the girls that he normally messed around with he couldn't deny her beauty. Even under those ugly clothes she was wearing.

"How old are you?" she asked him.

Even her voice was pretty. It was a little raspy but still delicate.

"Seventeen."

"Really? I've never seen you at school before," she let him know wide eyed. She would without a doubt remember if she had seen him around.

"I'm out here gettin' money baby girl. I don't have time for school."

The look on his face let her know that it wasn't a subject that he wanted to continue and neither did she.

Him not being in school and the fact that he was *gettin'
money* as he called it confirmed that he was into exactly
what she didn't want to be a part of. Even if she did want
to be a part of it her father would put an end to it before it
even started. There was no way that a pastor's daughter
was going to be with a drug dealer on his watch.

"Well we better get going. We have school
tomorrow and need to finish a project," Mila told the
little ugly dude.

"Beauty and brains. I like that," he said grinning
all up in her face and making her blush.

Haven wanted to throw up. Instead, she opted to
roll her eyes.

"Make sure you call me so we can get up," Mila
said and Haven's eyes almost bucked out of her head. If
her girl was planning on seeing Lil' Ugly again after they
left that meant that she would have to be around. Just like
always whenever Mila wanted to do something that she
had no business doing, Haven was her alibi. Just that
thought alone made her feel uncomfortable again.

"Yo, why you keep pulling at your clothes like that
Ma?" Asa asked her.

"Oh, umm just ready to get out of these clothes
that's all. It's hot," she lied. She wondered how it was
that he had picked up on what she was doing so easily

when most people didn't pay her enough attention to know what she did. Her father was always too busy with church business and saving souls and her mother hadn't had the opportunity to do anything with her. Having a heart attack at such a young age had caused Haven to learn how to be a woman all alone.

"Well we out," Asa told her. He tapped her lightly on her arm to get her attention before smiling and walking off. Within seconds the music that was playing had resumed and Mila was standing there smiling like she was in a Colgate commercial.

"Girl I'm 'bout to have all his babies," Mila said seriously.

"We need to go back to the church," Haven replied.

"For what? Why?"

"Cause obviously you need to go lay back on the altar and pray to God he gives you your sense back."

"Cut it out you know he's fine," Mila sassed in a playful manner.

"That boy was about as fine as the donkey that carried Mary to the manger," Haven laughed walking off towards their destination.

~4~

"I and my Father are one."

John 10:30

"Aye bruh, I'm 'bout to give shawty all my kids, feel me?" Fangas spoke while looking at Mila through the sideview mirror.

He rubbed his hands excitedly showing off a grin a mile wide.

"Yeah aight. Mess around and have Ina cut you again," Trouble told him referring to Fanga's girlfriend.

"Whatever man. What Ina don't know won't hurt her."

Instead of responding, Trouble just chuckled and shook his head. No matter what he said Fangas was gonna do what he wanted to anyway. He would just be ready to take his friend to the hospital when Ina found out like he knew she would.

"So what ya' old dude want?" Fangas asked getting serious.

Trouble remained in deep thought as he drove trying to figure out the same thing. He knew that it couldn't be about business because he was handling his areas like he was supposed to. When his father O'shea called him earlier he could hear anger in his voice but Trouble wasn't sure about who it was aimed at. He wasn't slipping as far as business was concerned so his mind kept drawing a blank.

"I don't even know. All he said was that we needed to fall through then he hung up."

Neither one of them spoke again caught up in their thoughts. Fangas with his mind on the young cutie he had just met and Trouble trying to think of everything possible that could be wrong and still drawing a blank.

Pulling up to the warehouse Trouble noticed the candy apple red Maserati parked next to his father's car and sucked his teeth. If that car was here then it meant that his father's trifling girlfriend Chinirika was there. If it was one person that Trouble hated more than anything it was her.

"Looks like step mama here," Fangas joked but Trouble found no humor in it.

On the outside of the building it looked like the warehouse was deserted but once you got behind the closed doors it was anything but. Naked women filled the huge space as they cooked, cut, and bagged up the product that O'shea flooded the streets with. If they weren't handling the drugs they were making sure the new shipments of guns were up to par.

Walking further into the large space Fangas licked his lips at all of the exposed bodies while Trouble ignored it. Women right now were a distraction for him and he had to stay on top of his game. That's why he couldn't understand why Haven was on his mind. She wasn't even his type. Heavyset and a church girl, not to mention he picked up on how insecure she was. He didn't have time to be coddling anyone when there was an empire to maintain.

Instead of knocking on his father's office door where he knew to find him, Trouble punched in the code for entry and walked in. Upon entering he wished he had knocked after finding O'shea in a compromising position with Chinirika's head in his lap. His father was such a savage that he didn't even flinch when he saw his son standing there.

"Either close my door and let me finish or have a seat," O'shea told him.

Fangas moved towards the couch in the office to take a seat but Trouble stopped him.

"For real bruh?"

"What? He gave us an option," Fangas replied genuinely confused and seeing nothing wrong with what he was about to do.

"Let's go," Trouble told him pushing him out the door.

It was another fifteen minutes before Chinirika emerged from the office looking unbothered as usual.

"Trifling," Trouble mumbled.

"Ya daddy like it," she replied.

Trouble watched her as she headed towards the exit in a pair of shorts that looked like they were painted on. He could never take away from her physical beauty because she was definitely a bad one. All he could think about though was how much he hated her. There was something about her that didn't sit well with him and he knew that she couldn't be trusted. There was no doubt that one day karma would find her. When that day came Trouble hoped he would be there to see her take her last breath.

Trouble removed his eyes from her body unlike Fangas who couldn't help himself. That was just too much woman for him not to look.

"I'm here so what's good? I got things to handle and sitting here is taking away from that," Trouble told O'shea.

The mug on his face matched the one that was looking back at him across the huge oak desk that sat between them.

"Lil' nigga don't get beside yourself," O'shea told him seriously.

Trouble saw Fangas shift uncomfortably in his seat through his peripheral and wanted to laugh. Out on the streets he acted so hard but when it came to O'shea he was quick to turn into a scared child. Trouble on the other hand paid it no mind. There was nothing that any man on the face of the earth could do to put fear in his heart. His father was ruthless but so was Trouble when he had to be. There had been plenty of times that the two men had come to blows with neither of them backing down. That's just how it was.

There had never been a time that O'shea and Trouble had a real father and son relationship. It was always business for him once he turned thirteen. The early part of his life Trouble lived with his grandmother and was afforded somewhat of a normal childhood. That was until one day when O'shea showed up on her doorstep and telling her it was time. Trouble didn't know what that meant then but obviously his beloved Granna did. She begged O'shea to let him stay and not expose him to that lifestyle but O'shea wasn't hearing that.

The last four years of Trouble's life consisted of him being right under O'shea's thumb. He drilled into him every day what he wanted Trouble to be like and so far, his plan had been working. O'shea was confident that Trouble would never betray him. Even if O'shea was the one that had been betraying Trouble since he was born.

"I need you to find her," O'shea told him sliding a picture across the desk towards Trouble and Fangas.

Looking down at the picture of the beauty Trouble was confused. Was this a trick of some kind to see if he still had his priorities in order or was it something else? O'shea was known to test people to see just how loyal they were to him and this felt like a set up to him.

"Aye! That's ole girl," Fangas yelled out excitedly. He nudged Trouble like he wasn't looking at the same picture and had figured out the same thing.

Ignoring his boy, Trouble looked back at his father.

"What you want with her?" he asked.

"I just need you to get close and get me some information," O'shea kept it vague.

"What kind of information?"

"We'll discuss that later. For now, get as close as you can and I'll take care of the rest. Now get up out my office and handle business."

Trouble could already sense there was something brewing that he wasn't sure if he wanted to be a part of but he also knew that he didn't have a choice in the matter. Either he did what he was told or deal with the consequences. The latter involved his Granna and he would go to war with O'shea if his threats were carried out.

Granna was Trouble's grandmother on his mother's side so O'shea didn't care what happened to her. He had made that clear many times before and that was one of the main reasons that Trouble did what he was told. If it wasn't for Granna, he would have been dead along with his mother. The same day that Lisa had dropped a two year old Asa off to her mother she was gunned down in the middle of Walmart.

O'shea was the reason that she was on the run and all she could think about was getting her baby boy somewhere safe. She had spent almost five years with the notorious O'shea Thomas and had finally gotten the nerve to leave. It was the brutal beating that she received at his hands that landed her in the hospital for almost a month. She had prayed that if God allowed her to live she would get as far from him as she could. Not only did her life depend on it but her young son's life as well.

The moment she was discharged from the hospital she had her so called best friend Chinirika take her to the bus station. Lisa begged Chinirika not to tell where she was going. Chinirika being the conniving snake that she was, looked her right in her face and promised knowing that she couldn't wait to tell O'shea. The bus hadn't even pulled out of the terminal good before she was heading over to the house her so called best friend shared with O'shea so that she could give up her whereabouts. She figured that if she showed her loyalty to O'shea he would finally make her his main lady. For years Chinirika felt that Lisa took O'shea from her and let her jealously get the best of her.

Granna was so relieved that her only daughter had finally come to her senses and left her no good boyfriend alone. She made sure that she had everything set up for Lisa and Asa. One of the ladies from her church owned a small dry cleaners and had agreed to give her a job. It wouldn't bring her anywhere near the money she was used to having but that didn't matter to her. All she cared about was making sure that she and her son got away.

When Lisa arrived with Asa she wished she had felt a sense of relief, instead an overwhelming sense of dread loomed over her. Granna was feeling the same way but she didn't say anything. She knew the type of man O'shea was and him just letting her go that easily was out of his character and she was right.

Hours after Lisa had gotten to Granna's house she realized there were some things that Asa needed that she didn't have. Granna begged her not to leave out but she promised to come right back since the store was less than a mile away. The whole time Lisa shopped she couldn't help but to feel like she was being watched. Looking around and not seeing anything out of the ordinary she decided to head to the toy section to get Asa a few toys. The moment she turned down the aisle she was met with a flurry of bullets. Before her body had the chance to hit the floor her spirit had already left her body.

Back at Granna's house there was a knock on the door. When she opened it she saw a tall dark skin man standing there looking even more sinister than she imagined Satan to look.

"Can I help you?" she asked with a shaky voice.

"Since Lisa went against the grain she had to be dealt with. If you don't want the same to happen to you I suggest you keep that mouth of yours shut," he told her before walking away and getting back into the car that was parked in her yard.

Granna didn't know what he meant but the chill that she felt go down her spine kept her frozen in place. She stood there so long with her eyes closed and praying that she hadn't even noticed when the two police cruisers pulled up until one of the officers spoke. As soon as he told her what had happened, her legs gave out on her and she went tumbling to the floor. The female officer that was there did her best to help console her while they tried to figure out if she knew who had killed her Lisa. Of course she knew who did it, but the whimpers coming from the couch that held her grandbaby caused her to tell them otherwise. She was positive that the police wouldn't have been able to save her had she told them the truth. Granna may not have been about that street life but she was no dummy. The code of the streets still applied and she couldn't chance something happening to Asa.

She prayed day in and day out that Asa would be covered in the blood of Jesus and no one came for him. For years she was constantly looking over her shoulders and just when she had begun to breathe a little easier and let her guard down O'shea showed up to take her baby. Her pleas not to take him fell on deaf ears so once again she got down on her knees and cried out to God that everything that she had instilled in Asa would not be in vain. She prayed that he would be one with his Father that was in heaven and not the one that walked the earth.

***

Trouble sat in the back of the trap house counting the last bit of money that one of the workers had dropped off. Although his count was on point his mind was still elsewhere. From meeting Haven weeks ago and then his father giving him a new task that he had no clue on what to do, his mind was boggled. He just couldn't understand why Haven's perfect smile kept flashing through his mental.

"What got you all googly eyed?" Fangas asked coming into the room.

"Huh?" Trouble was confused.

"You over there counting money and showing all your crooked teeth," Fangas laughed.

"Bruh you really want to go there about the teeth?" Trouble snapped back knowing good and well Fangas had no room to talk about anyone's teeth. The braces that he had worn for years had contributed to his perfect smile that drove the females crazy.

"That's cold man," Fangas replied like he was offended. He knew his grill was a mess but that never stopped him from getting the ladies anytime he wanted.

"So you got all the other spots?" Trouble wanted to know as he placed the last rubber band around the stack of money and placed it into the large duffle bag.

"You already know. We just need to put everything up then we straight."

"Bet."

Once they were done in the back the two of them made their way to the front to give orders and they were on their way.

"You get in touch with your next baby mama?" Trouble asked laughing.

"Man she been blowing ya boy up!" Fangas told him excitedly.

"Keep on and Ina gone blow you up for real."

Instead of responding, Fangas pecked away on his phone to let Mila know that they would be on the way soon. Since meeting her, Mila had been talking about what she wanted to do to him. He couldn't wait to see if she could back up everything she talked about. Clearly, she wasn't as innocent as her friend and that was just fine by him.

While Fangas sat in his seat thinking about all of the things he wanted to do to Mila, Trouble was trying to get his thoughts together. It confused him how his heart was fluttering at just the thought of seeing Haven again. They had only spent a few minutes in one another's presence and neither of them had any plans of seeing the other again. As luck, or God would have it, he was about to spend some much needed time with her. He just hoped that she would be just as excited to see him as he was to see her.

~5~

"Many daughters have done virtuously, but thou excellest them all."

Proverbs 31:29

"I'll be back in the morning baby girl," Hosea told his daughter with his overnight bag thrown across his shoulder.

Looking up from her notebook Haven took her glasses off before speaking.

"Again Daddy?"

"I know that you want me to stay here baby but you know I'm on assignment. I have to do the work of the Lord. That's what I was called to do," he said sighing. He hated that they had to have this conversation every weekend but there was nothing he could do about it. *His* ministry called.

"But Daddy your first ministry is home and you're barely here," she said hitting him what she knew to be true. For him to be spreading the gospel of Jesus he sure did forget that part.

"Ouch! Hit me with my own teachings then," he closed his eyes and grabbed his chest as if he was wounded. "I promise after this weekend I'll take some time off just for the three of us to hang out.

"Three of us?" Haven asked confused.

"Yeah. Me, you, and Shaunie," he told her like she should have known who he was talking about.

"I'll pass," she stated seriously returning her glasses to her face before looking at her notebook again.

There was no way that Haven would be spending any time with Shaunie no matter how badly she wanted to spend it with her father. She would just take the loss and maybe one day he would make time for her. If it wasn't the church, going on mission trips, or Shaunie, Hosea didn't have time for her. If she wanted that father daughter time then she would have to figure out a way to include herself in those activities. The more time that he was away the further apart they grew.

Alone time wouldn't have been so bad if she didn't get lost in her thoughts of her mother being gone and not really having anyone else besides Mila to express her feelings too. That was her girl and all but Mila wasn't always the best person to discuss her serious feelings with. There was no doubt in her mind that she would be there if Haven needed her to be, but sometimes Mila didn't think before she reacted. Either that or she wouldn't fully understand how she felt because Mila still had her mother. She may have been a ratchet mess but she was still there for her daughter come hell or high water. Tika was there for Haven too if she needed her even if she was extra all the time.

"When I ge-," Hosea started before Haven cut him off.

"Its fine Daddy. Have a good trip and be careful. I'll see you tomorrow night. I love you," she rushed out never taking the time to look up at him.

No matter what Haven may have thought, her father did love her and he wanted nothing more than to be there the way she needed him to be but he couldn't. At least not yet. One day he would be able to be the father she needed but right then he had to be the minister that the streets needed.

"We'll go shopping for your prom dress when I come back. Deal?" he asked with his voice full of hope.

"Mmm hmmm," was her only reply.

As excited as she should have been about prom she wasn't. No one had even bothered asking her and it was less than two months away and she wasn't even sure that if someone had, she would want to go. Things like that she should have been experiencing with the both of her parents, especially her mother. Haven hated to sound like she was complaining to God about this one subject so much but it hurt her to her core and she had no idea how to get past it.

Without another word, Hosea dropped his head and headed out to the garage. Deciding that she wouldn't be able to focus on the notes before her, Haven decided to put them up and get things ready for Mila to come over. Every weekend that her father was gone it was just the two of them. Laughing, eating, and catching up on their ratchet reality tv dramas. Hosea didn't want her watching tv through the week because he wanted her to be focused on school, so the weekend was her time to binge watch and catch up.

Just when Haven had taken the last of the wings out of the hot grease and placed them in her signature barbeque and lemon pepper sauce, the doorbell rang. She already knew that it was Mila so she hurried to let her in.

"Hey best fr-," Haven started and stopped abruptly when she saw that Mila wasn't alone.

"Hey chick!" Mila said excitedly and tried to rush past Haven.

"Unt uh," Haven told her while reaching her arm out to stop Mila from moving any further.

"So, what? You too good to let us in yo' house?" Fangas asked with his face balled up. When they pulled up to the house he could only imagine what the inside of the immaculate home looked like just by the way the outside looked.

The five bedroom, four bathroom sat on almost a half acre of land. The landscaping had to have been done on a regular basis by the looks of all of the colorful flowers that surrounded the front and the grass was cut. To him it looked more like a pimp or a kingpin's house than a pastor, but as he was taught pastors were pimps anyway so it was fitting.

"Listen Lil' Ugly. It has nothing to do with me being better than anyone but the fact that my daddy don't play these type of games. Mila you know if he came back here right now what would happen." Haven snapped causing Trouble to be unable to contain his laughter.

"That won't happen boo. The last thing yo' daddy would do is come back here especially with Shaunie in the car," Mila told her with a smirk on her face.

By the way Haven's face balled up she already knew that anger was setting in. It was one thing for her father to continually leave her alone for the weekend but to know that he was taking Shaunie with him was too much. She could slowly feel herself being over taken by rage and an uncaring attitude. The more he kept disappointing her the more she began to change and he didn't even know it. How could he when he was always focusing on everything and everyone else but her?

Instead of caring anymore, Haven threw caution to the wind and moved out of the way to give them room to enter.

"Girl you cooked my favorite wings?" Mila asked making a right leading into the kitchen area.

"Of course."

Before Haven could follow behind her Trouble reached out and grabbed her hand stopping her in her tracks. As soon as he touched her it was hard for Haven to keep her smile at bay. No matter how upset she was with Mila for not telling her that he was coming with Lil Ugly, she couldn't help but to be excited that Asa was there with her. Since they had met earlier in the week she found it hard to not think about him. Even at school her thoughts were consumed with images of his handsome face.

"Why you looking at me like that?" she asked him. Instantly she started fidgeting with the off the shoulder tee she wore over her short shorts. She would never wear anything like that out in public but when she was in the privacy of her own home she wanted to be comfortable. It was at that moment that he spoke when she realized what she was wearing.

"Stop doing that," Trouble told her while pulling her closer to him.

Oh God he smells so good, Haven thought. She couldn't help but to close her eyes and inhale his scent.

"Doing what?" she asked.

"Pulling on your clothes like that."

"I'm not," she lied with her head down.

Taking his index finger, he placed it under her chin and lifted her head until she looked at him with those gorgeous eyes of hers. Her heart was beating a mile a minute and she was beginning to get lightheaded. How and why was he having this effect on her? She hadn't known him long at all and this was only her second time seeing him in person. Unbeknownst to Haven he was having the same thoughts and he didn't understand what was going on.

"I'll help break you out of that sooner or later," Trouble assured her. Winking his eye at her he gave that killer heart fluttering smile and walked off in the direction that he saw Mila and Fangas walk.

Haven stood there stuck on stupid and thinking about everything that could possibly go wrong. Her father coming home to find boys in their house, something coming up broken or missing, and most importantly the feelings down below that were about to consume her. God knows she was trying to put her flesh under subjection but the way Trouble had her feeling, she knew that being around him would be just that. *Trouble.*

Forgetting about all of the things that could possibly go wrong, Haven decided to enjoy the moment as much as she could because if her daddy came home she knew for a fact that she wouldn't see the light of day after that. If she was going to be locked down then she might as well go out with a bang.

Entering the kitchen she saw Trouble, Mila, and Fangas with food in front of them in front of the bar area.

"Asa would you like something to drink?" she asked calling him by his birth name.

Unlike Mila and Fangas, Trouble was waiting on Haven to join them before he began eating. His stomach was growing something horrible because he had gone all day without eating. Picking up money, dropping off drugs, and occasionally having to get one of the workers back in line he didn't have the time. As soon as Haven opened the door and the aroma of hot and fresh chicken hit his nose he prayed that before she made them leave that he could get a to go plate. Thankfully God was on his side. From her house back to the nearest fast food joint it would have been a minute and he wasn't gonna make it.

Speaking of God, the guilt about how he lived his life was starting to get to him and all he could think about was how coming across Haven had done something to him. Thoughts of everything that Granna had taught him came rushing back when he met Haven. They hadn't been around each other long but it was enough to make him want to be.

"Oh so you see us sitting here and the only one you ask if they thirsty is this fool?' Fangas asked.

"Well since we don't have any Proactive cocktails to clean up that face of yours from the inside…" Haven commented.

Before Fangas could respond Trouble was about to pass out from laughing. The way his voice sounded when he laughed made her feel all giddy inside and she couldn't help but to cross her arms and shift her weight to the other foot.

"Now sis you can't be getting on my boo like that. He may look like a star crunch snack but that's bae," Mila took up for him causing both Haven and Trouble to laugh harder.

"See that's why you gonna be my baby mama one day. Taking up for your man and all," Fangas confessed.

"Ohhhh Mi you can get one from overseas," Haven hinted.

Moving from the fridge with two cold cherry Pepsi's in her she handed Trouble one and sat down on the empty seat beside him. It was taking everything in her power not to laugh at the confused looks on everyone's face because they didn't know what she meant.

"Get what from overseas?" Mila asked.

"A baby. Because a baby by that one there," she began while pointing her finger at Fangas, "is not the move. The hospital gonna call the zoo so fast when that baby pops out and tell them one of their lil' orangutans escaped."

Trouble had just opened his soda and put the can to his lips taking a big swig before spitting it all out across the floor. He didn't know what was funnier, the fact that she told them flat out that their baby would be ugly or because it was true. Mila was a cute girl but Fangas had some strong genes. His whole family was a sight to see and not in a good way. If anything, Trouble had to agree with Haven but he wouldn't tell his boy that.

"Man shut yo' fat-," Fangas began. Everything was all cool a minute ago but now he crossed the line.

"Hold up bruh," Trouble said getting serious and cutting him off at the same time Mila spoke.

"Not that one right there," Mila fumed tilting her head towards a sad looking Haven. Neither Trouble or

Fangas knew the battle that Haven dealt with on the daily because of her size and although she had taken up for him there was no way that she was going to sit back and let him get on her best friend.

"So you gonna take up for her?" Fangas asked.

"Please believe it! That's a lifetime bond my boy and you just got here."

"I'll be back," Haven mumbled before a tear fell down her face. She tried to wipe it quickly and not have her voice shake but she was failing. She needed to get to her safe place and regroup.

"You foul for that bruh," Trouble spoke up. The moment the insult left Fanga's lips he felt her body stiffen. She was sitting close enough to him for their arms to touch and before he could reach for her she was making her way out of the room.

"Wait a minute you on her side too? We supposed to be boys," Fangas reminded Trouble.

"We are," Trouble fumed and got up.

"Let me go check on her," Mila told them and rolled her eyes.

"Nah let me," Trouble offered.

Mila thought for a moment about his request and for a moment she was unsure. She was her sister's keeper and that would always come first. Just as she was about to decline a thought crossed her mind. Although they hadn't known one another long maybe it would be good for Haven to hear something positive from someone else.

"Top of the stairs make a left. Her room is the only room on that side of the house," she informed him.

The hunger pangs Trouble was just experiencing had disappeared and the only thing he could think of was to make sure that Haven was good. There was a rack at the bottom of the stairs that held shoes so he assumed that he was to take his off before heading up.

There were frames all along the wall of Haven as a small child and throughout the years of her growing up. What stuck out to him was the fact that none of them contained a woman just a man that he assumed was her father.

Knocking on the door lightly Trouble waited for her to acknowledge him. When she didn't answer after the third time he reached for the doorknob and thankfully it was unlocked. When he opened the door he was stuck in amazement for a few moments at how nice her room was. The whole left side of the house belonged to Haven. His room at home was big but not that big.

Haven had a bed in the middle of her room that was so large he knew about six people could rest comfortably there with no problem. Her 60" inch television hung on her wall in front of the bed. Beside it was a dresser that resembled a *Bath and Body Works* display because there were so many bottles of perfume, lotion, and shower gels.

"I wanna see you, no distractions, I wanna know you're here," Haven sang through sniffles.

Stopping his observation of her room, he wondered where her voice was coming from. She wasn't on the bed or sitting on the deep purple chaise lounge that sat in front of the large window. It was then that he noticed a door slightly ajar with a light illuminating from it. Hoping it was her closet and not her bathroom he walked over to it slowly. Through the crack he could see clothes hanging up so he knew that was the closet.

Trouble stopped in his tracks when Haven came into view and his breath got stuck in his throat. Looking at her balled up on the floor with her eyes closed and tears falling like rain made him wish that he had let Mila come check on her instead. This was something that he wasn't used to doing. He was in the streets heavy thanks to his old man and compassion was something that he never gave to anyone besides his grandmother.

Tasha Cobb's song *"Here"* played along as Haven sang along in one of the most beautiful voices he had ever heard besides his mother. No matter how long she had been gone he can remember how her voice sounded whenever she would sing him to sleep. It was the one memory that he had prayed never left him.

Haven was so into her worship that she didn't know she that she was no longer alone. Trouble stood at the entrance to the closet until she let out a gut wrenching cry that penetrated his own spirit. Without a second thought he moved closer to sit down beside her and touched her hand. Haven's eyes popped open and she jumped.

"I didn't mean to scare you," he let her know.

There were no words that Haven spoke as she sat up and leaned against the wall. For almost twenty minutes the two of them just sat in their own thoughts before Trouble's voice filled the space.

"You good?" he asked.

Nodding her head, Haven fiddled with her shirt. Trouble saw it and reached out to move her hand away from it. He hated she did that. After he removed her hand from her clothes he extended his towards her chin and once again lifted her head. She looked so sad and broken with her red eyes staring back at him.

"I know you might not think so right now but Fangas didn't mean nothing by what he said. You just crushed his manhood about his future child no matter how true it is."

That time Trouble was able to get somewhat of a response from her in the form of a light laugh.

"What are those?" he asked her looking at all of the small notes that were attached to her back wall. The closet was so big and they were so far away he couldn't make out what was written on them.

"My writings on the wall."

Directing his attention back to her with a confused expression on his face he waited for her to explain.

"Those are all of my prayer requests."

"You mean like from that movie where that old lady was in the closet all the time? She taught some woman how to pray," he recalled.

"War Room."

"That's it! My Granna made me go see that with her when it first came out. I wasn't tryna go but she wasn't having that."

"Sounds like she doesn't play."

"Not even the radio," He said making them both laugh.

"I wish I had someone that cared enough to spend some time with me like that. You're lucky," she expressed.

"From the pictures in the hall it looks like you had a pretty good life," Trouble revealed to her.

"Money and materialistic things don't move me. My dad is too focused on doing ministry and being there for everybody else that he uses stuff to fill the void I guess," Haven confessed.

"Where's your old lady?"

"Huh?"

Trouble laughed at her confusion before explaining that was his term for mother. Once she understood she filled him in.

"She died when I was three. It's been me and my dad since."

"Mine died when I was two."

"Oh wow. I'm sorry for your loss. I guess we do have something in common after all."

"Looks like it."

"How did she pass?" Haven wanted to know.

"Shot at a Walmart. They never found out who did it." Sadness was etched across his handsome face and for a moment Haven forgot about her issues.

"That's tough. Not knowing why."

"What about yours?"

"She had cervical cancer from what my dad told me. No one ever knew that she had it until it was too late. By then no treatment would work so it was a waiting game. Daddy said that he had gone on a weekend retreat that she insisted he go on and when he got there something didn't feel right so he headed back home. When he got there she was gone."

"Dang shawty that's messed up."

"It's his MO and now I'm used to it. Nothing comes before his work for the Lord," she told him in a disgusted tone and using her fingers to draw air quotes.

"That's why I can't get down with all that church stuff. Too many fakes and people lying about what thus said the Lord. Don't get me wrong I believe in God but people will have you questioning some things."

"That's why we have to know God for ourselves. When that time comes no one's opinion about you or what they did will get you into heaven. You riding solo dolo."

"*Solo dolo?*" Trouble mocked.

"Hush," Haven fussed.

Ringing could be heard coming from the other side of the closet so Haven stood up to go and get it. By the ringtone alone she already knew that it was her daddy calling. Not in the mood to talk to him right then Haven didn't even want to answer but she knew if she didn't it wouldn't take long for him to call one of the church mothers to come and check on her.

Haven remembered one time where she was asleep and her phone had died. She woke up to someone pounding on the door like the police and ringing the bell simultaneously. It had startled her so bad that she didn't quite register where she was right away. Once she knew she was home alone she rushed down the stairs almost falling and breaking her neck, thinking something was wrong with her daddy.

The moment she opened the door to see Mother Easley standing there her heart dropped to her feet thinking her assumptions were correct. Mother Easley killed that theory the minute she put her cell phone to her ear and told who she learned was her daddy, that she must have been in there with a boy. That old woman checked every nook and cranny in their spacious home looking for a boy that wasn't there. Every time she bent down Haven could hear her knees popping like some pop rocks candy. It would have been funny if her daddy wasn't so upset that she missed all of his calls. He fussed for what seemed like forever about her being responsible and making sure her phone stayed charged in case of emergencies. That was something that she didn't want to happen again especially with her uninvited guests.

"Hey daddy. I'm fine," Haven greeted but didn't receive a response. "Daddy?"

Pulling the phone from her ear she saw that the call was still connected but he had yet to say anything.

"Helloooo?"

Thinking that he must have butt dialed her Haven got ready to hand up. Before she could tap the red button on her phone what she heard next stopped her dead in her tracks.

"Did you tell her yet?" Haven heard Shaunie ask instantly turning her mood even more sour than before.

"Not yet," Hosea replied.

"Well you don't have long cause I refuse to walk down the aisle with a big stomach and I am not bringing this baby into the world unmarried," Shaunie sassed.

Baby? Marriage? Haven thought to herself. She had to be hearing things. There was no way that her daddy was about to marry Shaunie knowing how much she despised the woman and the feeling was definitely mutual. It wasn't like she wanted him to be alone for the rest of his life but she knew that Shaunie wasn't the one. Now she was about to be a big sister and he didn't even bother to tell her.

Just that fast the enemy had come to steal the prayers that she had just let out and Haven was livid. Not bothering to listen to anything else because she had heard enough, Haven hung up the phone just as Trouble came out of the closet to see what was going on and Mila entered the room with Fangas behind her.

"Aye my bad about earlier," Fangas lied. He didn't care one bit about how he had hurt Haven's feelings because she came at him first. But if he wanted to see Mila perform that special trick she told him about he would apologize. As fine and freaky as she claimed to be he would vote for Trump again just to appease her.

"You good. Mila you got some twerk juice?" Haven asked seriously.

Mila's eyes got as wide as saucers upon hearing her best friend asking for her signature mixture of alcohol and some other stuff. Whatever she put in there always had her lifted but Haven never participated. So to hear her ask for some things must have been bad. There was no way that the comment Fangas said to her caused her to go off the deep end like that.

"Sis you sure?" Mila inquired.

"Girl yes or no?" Haven found herself getting beyond irritated and wished that Mila would hurry up and give her what she had asked for. If not things were about to turn up and not in a good way.

Deciding that the look Haven was giving her, Mila told them to follow her downstairs where she had put it in the freezer to get cold. She couldn't even get the door to the freezer open good before Haven reached over her and pulled out the Sprite bottle. Haven was so in need that she wasted no time unscrewing the top and taking it to the head.

"Hay! Slow down girl. You gotta go easy on that before you be flat on your behind," Mila warned.

Haven ignored her before doing something that shocked everyone in the room. She walked up to Fangas and retrieved the pre rolled blunt that was behind his ear.

"Aye man!" Fangas yelled out.

Still paying them no mind, it didn't take long to find a lighter because Mila carried one at all times. With the grape flavored cigarillo to her lips Haven lit it up and took a long pull on it and held it in like she knew what she was doing.

"Jesus!" Haven called out the best she could through her coughing fit. It felt like her lungs were about to explode and her eyes were watering as she tried to catch her breath.

"Look at cha! Bout to kill yo'self trying to hang with the big boys," Trouble joked.

If they thought that Haven was done surprising them they were sadly mistaken. She even shocked herself when Trouble closed in the space between them to make sure she was alright. Haven wrapped her arms around his neck and stood on her tip toes before covering his lips with hers. Not a day since she had been alive had she kissed a man other than her daddy and this was nothing like those pecks on his cheeks. This was a grown woman kiss. That twerk juice mixed with the potent weed in her system and Trouble looking like a snack caused Haven to step outside of her comfort zone. If only for one night she wanted to forget about her dead mama, her lying daddy, and the low self-esteem that consumed her daily.

When she broke the intense kiss she looked into Trouble's eyes and hoped that he knew what was on her mind. If he didn't she didn't mind showing him. Dropping her arms, she reached for his hand that was sitting on her lower back and walked around Mila and Fangas like they weren't even there.

Fangas made eye contact with Trouble before discretely nodding his head. This was about to be easier than he had initially thought. He was hoping that Trouble was about to live up to his name and cause more trouble than Haven could have ever anticipated.

~6~

"Woe to the rebellious children, saith the Lord..."
Isaiah 30:1

That first night with Trouble didn't only have Haven's nose wide open but other parts of her body as well that shouldn't have been. She had gone from the good little church girl to hell on wheels in hopes that her father would take notice. Skipping school some days, smoking weed on the regular, and even a change in her wardrobe didn't even cause him to bat an eye because he was so focused on other things and people. Shaunie in particular. So instead of making a big deal about it, she decided to focus all of her time on the one man that had yet to disappoint her.

Trouble had been with her every day and she was loving every minute with him. He was enjoying her company way more than he should have considering he wasn't one to have ever been in a committed relationship. He knew what was to come but there was no turning back. The moment he was allowed to meet her in her intimate place things changed. Not just for him but her as well.

Haven was slowly turning into the bad girl that she really wasn't and Trouble was starting to feel a tug on his heart in another direction. The shy and insecure girl that he had met had done a number on him and she didn't even know it. It made him think about all of the times that he was growing up and Granna told him that when God presented his wife to him that he would know. There would be no doubt in his mind or heart who she was and he was now thinking that time had come. His newfound angel had come in and unknowingly sparked something in him. He just prayed that his somewhat negative influence on her could be undone. Deep down they both knew that wasn't who she really was and she was just lashing out to make her father pay attention to her. Since he wasn't, Trouble decided that he would be what she needed him to be. At seventeen years old, it was now time for him to be that man Granna and his mother wanted him to be for real. No more lies and no more games. That was why he made up in his mind as soon as he got the chance that night he was telling her everything.

"Tonight's the night bruh," Fangas told Trouble getting his attention.

The two of them were just about to head out of the house and head over to Haven's church. It was her prom night and she had asked him to go with her. It wasn't his scene but he had to bite the bullet. He had been putting off what his father wanted him to do but O'shea had given him an ultimatum that if he didn't handle his business then O'shea would be forced to take matters into his own hands. After tonight there was no turning back. Trouble wasn't sure that he could get away with it but his newfound faith in God gave him a glimmer of hope.

Things had changed drastically in just a couple of months but it was clear that he needed to find a way out. One night while he was spending time with Haven at her house Trouble made his way into her closet. After the first time of him being there, each time he came over there was a tug on his heart. Finally getting up the nerve he chose that night to go with his gut. While Haven was in the shower he slipped in and closed the door behind him. The undeniable power was so strong that it caused him to lean against the closed door for support.

Once he got himself together he moved closer to the many pieces of paper that covered her wall. He laughed inwardly when he thought about the scene in War Room where the woman's husband entered his wife's room for the first time. He read over a few before one in particular caught his eye. Trouble knew that it had to have been new because of the brightness of the paper. All of the other ones were worn out and dingy.

God I know I've disappointed you with some of my actions and there are no excuses so please forgive me. I don't know why Asa was brought into my life but I am so

*thankful for him. I recognize that you used him to help
me with my inner battles. Probably unbeknownst to him.
So I ask that you use me to help him. There are so many
things about Him that I don't know but you do. The trials
and tribulations only come to make him stronger. Touch
his heart God so that he knows he is more than a
conqueror. You created him for your glory and as young
as we are I can see the calling that you have over his life.
Now let him see it and walk in it. No matter if this
relationship goes any further or not, please let us always
remain friends. I find your strength in him. I find your
peace in him. I feel your love in him. Let him find you in
me as well. Whatever your will for our lives are I thank
you in advance.*

Trouble stood there not realizing that tears were
flowing down his face until Haven touched his arm ever
so gently. Looking over at her she gave him a loving
smile. It was then that he felt love like never before. He
didn't even try to compose himself as his knees gave out
under him and he landed on the floor.

"God I'm sorry! Help me and guide me in your
ways. God, I ask for forgiveness of my many sins. I
know this life isn't what you had planned for me but I
pray that I can make a change now. I ask that you come
into my heart and lead me in the way that You will have
me to go. Only you can make this right. Please cover and

protect both Haven and me. In Jesus' name, Amen," Trouble cried out.

He didn't know if the words he felt in his heart that were now coming out of his mouth were correct but Trouble had to get them out. By the time he had gathered himself his body felt drained and the burden that weighed him down for years was gone. Finally he knew freedom.

It was then that he knew what he had to do but before he could his phone chimed. Just like he had heard Granna say many times before, the devil will come quick to steal your joy just as soon as you get it. His father's number showing up on his phone symbolized just that. Only that time he wouldn't succeed.

"I need to talk to you when I get back ok?" Trouble spoke.

"Ok," Haven replied. He picked up on her nervousness immediately and wanted to make sure she knew nothing was wrong.

"Don't worry Hay. I just want to open up and put everything on the table. Being here has awaken something in me and it's only right."

Nodding her head she let out the breath she was holding in and smiled again. That smile was everything to him and Trouble prayed that he could continue to see it after he laid it all out there.

"You hear me?" Fangas asked for the third time. Trouble had been so deep in his thoughts that he wasn't paying his boy any attention. Honestly, he wished that he would hush so that he could get his thoughts together but that wasn't about to happen.

Trouble was so tired of hearing the same things over and over about him getting his head in the game and if Fangas didn't stop he wasn't going to like what came out of Trouble's mouth.

"Yeah man, dang! I said I got this so fall back," Trouble barked.

Not one to want to get on Trouble's bad side Fangas backed off. Trouble may not have been a hot head like his father but when pushed too much he could definitely make people feel his wrath.

"Aiight, let's be out."

On the way to the front door O'shea heard them coming down the steps and stood up from his seat. He wanted to make sure that his son was on point and if not he would have to be made an example of. O'shea didn't care that Trouble was his flesh and blood. As far as he was concerned, everyone was disposable and if Trouble didn't execute the plan that he had set in motion by the end of the next day then O'shea would handle everyone accordingly.

Trouble had a feeling that he wouldn't be able to get out of the house without running into his father and by the look on his face he already knew what was up.

"I said I got it," Trouble assured him.

O'shea stood there looking at his first born intently. He was the spitting image of O'shea's father which caused his hatred for the man that brought him in the world to surface. The grimace displayed across his face was enough to let Trouble know he wasn't about to take it easy if he failed his mission. He could enjoy himself as a teenager that night but he better remember what his purpose was. The day Asa turned thirteen he became Trouble and was no longer a child in O'shea's eyes.

"You better or you know what will happen if not."

Trouble decided not to even dignify that statement with a response. Ignoring O'shea he turned to walk to the kitchen to retrieve the corsage that he had for Haven. He may not have been the romantic type but he knew a little something. If things were to go good that night he needed to come somewhat correct.

Because Trouble was no longer in the room O'shea made it his business to make sure that his plan was a success.

"Don't let me down tonight. Remember if you pull this off there's a position right next to me. We know that nigga ain't cut out for this. Once this is all done you know what to do," O'shea spoke to Fangas.

Fangas already knew how things were going to play out and he was all for it. What Trouble didn't know was that his loyalty wasn't to him but to his father. O'shea had been the one to save him from the dysfunctional family that he grew up with. When Fangas was just nine years old he met O'shea. He was trying to sell anything he could to get some money to buy a hot meal. Once again his parents had smoked up all of their food by selling their food stamps for dope. It had been almost a week since he had anything more than a bag of chips and a soda that he had stolen from the corner store. The way his stomach was hurting from being hungry he was desperate and O'shea played on that.

For a few days O'shea had been seeing Fangas out trying to sell an old busted up radio and approached him. Once he found out why he needed the money, O'shea broke off three hundred dollars and handed it to him. From that day forward Fangas was dedicated and loyal to only one person and that was the one that saved him. So if Trouble slipped up he wouldn't have a problem relieving him from his duties. He knew that Trouble was starting to have his judgement clouded by Haven so it would only be a matter of time before he came to the end of the road.

"Let's be out," Trouble told Fangas.

After discretely nodding his head at O'shea, Fangas followed Trouble out the door to the waiting limo that would be taking them to the church. Haven's dad decided to have a prom send off, whatever that was, at the church since there were quite a few seniors that were going to prom. It would also be the first time that Trouble met Haven's father. They had been kicking it heavy since the day he showed up at her house and her dad still didn't know about the relationship that had formed. For all he knew Trouble was someone that she went to school with and had asked her to prom. If that was the story that she wanted to go with who was he to go against it.

"You know that you need to put on your good boy act right?" Trouble asked.

"Go 'head with that bruh. I know what to do. You just make sure that you do what you supposed to," Fangas snapped back.

For the second time that day Trouble decided to ignore a statement and sit in his thoughts as they rode. He didn't know why but he was starting to regret his decisions in the worst way. What if things got out of hand? What if he went to jail? So many questions ran through his mind but the most important one was why did he have to go to these extremes? To that day O'shea still didn't tell them what was so important that he had to go to that school and wreak havoc on an innocent life or lives. Blood would be shed no doubt there was nothing he could do about it.

Trouble was snatched from his thoughts the moment they pulled up to the church. The parking lot was full of cars like it was a Sunday morning and he shook his head. Looking all of the of the smiling people he thought about how soon those smiles would be wiped off of their faces.

"Showtime," Fangas said breaking the silence and opening the door. Trouble took a deep breath and rubbed his arm where the scripture that was inked into his skin was covered by his shirt and jacket.

"I will fear no evil for thou art with me," he mumbled.

Getting out and closing the door behind him, Trouble noticed something in the parking lot that halted his steps. With a confused look on his face he stared in the direction of what caught his attention. Something was off or maybe it wasn't what he thought at all. Shaking off the feeling he headed inside to find his date.

~7~

"And many false prophets shall rise, and shall deceive many."

Matthew 24:11

Haven and Mila stood inside of the church bathroom with a few of the other girls that went to their school. Making sure she was put together she looked over her hair, makeup, and dress once more.

"Girl stop you look good and Asa is going to love it," Mila assured her friend. She didn't want to call Trouble by his street name because there was no telling if it would get back to Haven's father. The last thing she wanted was for him to make her girl stay away from him.

It was because of him that Haven had finally come out of her shell and started to enjoy life as a teenager instead of an old lady. She had even started to dress differently. Sadly, her father hadn't noticed the changes. He was too occupied with church business and sniffing behind Shaunie. Considering their relationship was this big secret, Haven still hadn't revealed to him that she knew about them. Shaunie didn't live there and she never spent the night so Hosea thought he was in the clear.

Instead of going off like she wanted to Haven decided to flip the script. If it wasn't for Trouble she would have been in a deep depression but he paid so much attention to her that he became her beautiful distraction.

"You're right let's go."

Picking up her cell phone, Haven checked the time and sent a text to see if their dates had arrived. Before she could pull up the text thread for Trouble there was an incoming message from him.

"They here," she told Mila before they walked out.

"My God you look beautiful baby girl," Hosea told Haven.

"You girls look great," Shaunie acknowledged with a smirk on her face.

Shaunie may have had her daddy fooled but not Haven or Mila. They knew she was just saying that to please him and it wasn't genuine.

"Thank you Daddy."

"I know you heard Shaunie compliment you. Don't be rude," Hosea chastised Haven.

"Our dates are here," Haven ignored him and walked off.

Hosea stood there in disbelief watching her walk away. It wasn't a secret that Haven had always despised

Shaunie but lately it had gotten worse. Instead of going after her and getting on to her he took a deep breath and walked behind her.

"You just gonna let her disrespect me like that?" Shaunie asked with her hands on her hips and a frown on her face.

"Baby let me deal with it later," he told her.

The moment Haven and Mila came into view Haven felt like all eyes were on her. Especially Trouble's. He couldn't lie, she looked amazing in her floor length black dress that revealed all of her curves. On her feet were a pair of black open toed heels that fastened around her ankles. She had her hair cut in golden layers that fell to the middle of her back and her makeup was flawless. If he wasn't captivated by her beauty before he definitely was then.

Mila wasn't too bad either and Fangas found it hard not to stare. Her dress was somewhat similar to what Haven was wearing except it was a royal blue and she had her hair cut short in finger waves. If he didn't already have a baby mama that Mila had no clue about, it would be nothing for him to make sure she was the one to give him a child. Although Mila was falling for him no matter how many times she denied it, the feeling was not mutual. All he wanted was one thing and she had given him that long ago.

"Hey pretty," Trouble told Haven.

"Hey handsome." She couldn't help but to blush and admire him as he took her hand and began to place the corsage around her wrist.

"Where mine at?" Mila asked Fangas.

"Outside on that rose bush y'all got on the side of the building," he told her not understanding the big deal.

"Really?"

"Come on man what I look like paying for some flowers to go around your arm and they gonna be dead before the end of the night? You got me messed up. You lucky I got dressed up."

"Ugh you make me sick. Come on so you can meet my mama and we can go," Mila ordered. She pulled his arm and walked off in the direction that she last saw her mother.

"Ahem," someone cleared their throat behind Haven and Trouble causing them to turn around. When they did Trouble locked eyes with the person that he had hoped wouldn't be there.

"Daddy this is Asa. Asa this is my daddy, Pastor Hosea Reynolds."

"Nice to meet you sir," Trouble greeted.

Hosea extended his hand to shake Trouble's before introducing Shaunie.

"Nice to meet you young man. This is Shaunie."

"Hi," Shaunie spoke up before excusing herself. She didn't even give him time to greet her before she went back in the direction that she had just come from.

"So you go to school with the girls?"

"Yes sir. We're in the same grade and take a few classes together," Trouble lied. He and Haven had already come up with the lie that they would tell in order for Hosea not to have any suspicions. He made sure that none of his tattoos would show and he didn't have his gold slugs in that he wore on occasion.

"What are your grades like Asa?"

"Daddy do we have to do this right now? I take all honors classes and Asa has three of them with me. That should tell you how his grades are," Haven snapped.

Reaching out for her hand and placing it in his he smiled at her.

"It's ok Hay," he told her before turning his attention to Hosea. "I'm an honor student since the eighth grade. Before then I was a little rebellious in school and acting out because I missed my mama but then my grandmother explained to me how important school was and I got it together."

The way that bold face lie slid off his tongue Haven almost believed it herself and from the looks of it her daddy was pleased with his answer.

"Very good. Maybe one day we can have you over to the house for dinner and get to know each other a little better. I know you are anxious to get going."

Shaking hands once again they all walked off to go and take pictures in front of the church before heading over to the school. While they did that Shaunie was rushing to get her phone out of her purse and place a call before anyone came looking for her.

"Hello?"

"We got a problem."

~8~

"Charm is deceptive and beauty is fleeting..."

Proverbs 31:30

"Everybody is gone so let's hurry up," Hosea told Shaunie coming into his office. He made sure that the coast was clear before locking up the church and rushing to handle business in the back.

Hosea took off his suit jacket along with his dress shirt and pushed the button under his desk that opened the secret room behind his book case. No one knew that was there except Shaunie considering she was the one that helped him take care of business.

When the case slid completely to the side he punched in the code in order to open the door. The moment he stepped across the threshold of the room he went from the preaching the paint-off-the-wall pastor to the pistol-toting-drug-slinging kingpin that no one knew about.

That church life that so many thought he was really about had him on a one way trip straight to hell. He didn't care as long as his work was flooding the streets so that his bank account could swell. He wasn't even ordained to be a deacon let alone a pastor. It was all a front to cover up what he really did so that he wouldn't raise any red flags with the law. He had been in this game for almost twenty five years and he wasn't giving it up any time soon.

Looking around at the spacious room in the back of the church he admired the many keys of uncut heroin and coke stacked neatly ready for him to distribute. Hosea didn't trust anyone to break down his supply in a church because he didn't want someone to notice all of the traffic in and out of the building. If people on the outside started seeing different people coming and going it would raise questions that he didn't want to answer.

"What's wrong with you?" Hosea asked Shaunie. She had an expression on her face that he couldn't read.

"Nothing," she stated in a flat tone.

Reaching out for her arm he pulled her close to him.

"You mad about me not telling Haven about the baby and my engagement?" he inquired.

If Hosea knew what she was really thinking then he would know that marrying him and having the baby that was growing in her stomach was the last thing on her mind. Her nerves were shot and it was taking everything in her power not to show the fear that she was feeling. Her mama had always told her that she would reap what she sowed be it good or bad. It was at that moment when she saw Trouble standing in that church that she knew she was about to reap a harvest full of hell.

"I know what you need," Hosea moaned against her neck. She could feel her body beginning to react to him but she couldn't focus so she faked.

Hosea led her over to the wall and kissed her. His mind was focused on reassuring her that he would deal with Haven while hers was focused on how she was going to make it out of that situation alive. There was no doubt in her mind that Trouble was going to blow her cover. That would be the day that Hosea learned that Shaunie never existed and it was Chinirika that he had made his ride-or-die chick.

***

Brianna sat silently in the last stall of the women's bathroom waiting for everyone to go on about their business. She was tired of beating around the bush with Hosea and it was time to make him hers. The first day that she had stepped her pretty feet inside of that church and saw him standing behind the pulpit she was committed to making him hers. If it wasn't for Shaunie always being around and ruining her moment they would have been married long ago.

"I bet I get him tonight," she told herself out loud.

Checking out the short shorts that exposed just the right amount of skin and the low cut blouse she wore there was no way that he could resist. Her body looked like something those Instagram models had to buy but she was all natural. Every man that came in contact with her wanted her but she wanted him. Hosea Reynolds was about to make her his first lady if it killed her.

She opened the bathroom door and stuck her head out to listen. Brianna wanted to be positive that they were alone and no one would see her. The bathroom that she was in was in the very back by his office so she didn't have to go far. Before anyone could even see down the hall to where she was, she would be inside of his office.

Looking around one last time she quickly turned the doorknob and was thankful that it was unlocked. As soon as she got on the other side and locked the door she heard what sounded like moans. That was when Brianna noticed the opening in the wall. She had been in that office countless times and never thought anything was behind it. Why would she? It was just a book case.

Now moving slowly trying not to make any noise, Brianna was just inches away from the door. Listening intently she tried her hardest to decipher who the moans belonged to.

"Shoot!" she whispered when she bumped into the desk. Frozen for what seemed like forever, Brianna let out the breath she was holding in. Once she was confident that they didn't hear her she proceeded on.

Had she known what was on the other side of that door she would have never stayed behind. Watching the back of Hosea's body in sync with Shaunie's wasn't what made her sick to her stomach. It was the sight of seeing all of the drugs and money that was spread out around them.

"Oh God."

That time she didn't whisper and immediately got the attention of Hosea and Shaunie. Before he could let Shaunie down onto her feet and buckle his pants Brianna was running at full speed trying to get away. She had no idea what was going on but what she did know was that the man that she had wanted to be her husband and leader was nothing but the devil. All of those years he stood in front of thousands of people claiming to preach the gospel when in all actuality he was doing nothing more than preaching lies.

The alarm blaring in the church let Hosea know that Brianna had already gotten outside of the building. Before he went to his office earlier he made sure to arm it so that he would be aware if anyone was present.

"Call Meech," was all Hosea said to Shaunie and she knew what that meant.

Doing as she was told she placed the call. Meech was the one who handled any problems that needed to be solved. Brianna may have escaped from Hosea at that moment but what was waiting on her at home would be ten times worse and she didn't even know it. All she could think about was getting home to get her most valuable possessions, throwing them in her car, and getting out of town. With what she saw she knew there was no way that Hosea wouldn't come after her. She may not have known what he was into but it was something and finding out what it was just wasn't on her bucket list of things to do.

Surprisingly she made it to her small house in record time without the police pulling her over. She couldn't help but to look around and check out her surroundings. With her hands shaking, her legs getting weak with every step she took, and her heart about to beat out of her chest she made it to her door.

"Come on!" Brianna fussed at herself when she dropped her keys to the ground.

Sliding the key into her lock and turning it, she let out a sigh of relief and unbeknownst to her Brianna rushed to her death. The bullet that exited the gun Meech was holding connected with Brianna's head before she even had time to realize what was happening. No one understood how Meech operated and how quickly he got things done. It had only been a short time ago that he received the call but he had already made his way inside of Brianna's house unnoticed.

Meech surveyed the scene that he had created to make it look like a robbery gone wrong before leaving out the same way he had come in. Normally when Hosea put out a hit he made sure to that the body was disposed of but not this time. He had a better idea that would allow him to cover his tracks.

~9~

"He sent His word and healed them, and delivered them from their destructions." Psalms 107:20

Haven had been complimented all night on how pretty she was and it was something that she wasn't used to. Trouble kept telling her the same thing all night but when he did it she felt like he meant it. Everybody else saw her day in and day out at school and never even bothered really talking to her. It wasn't that she didn't have friends because she did but they weren't as popular as the ones that had been in her face all night. The girls wanted to linger too long around her and Trouble and it was starting to annoy her.

Trouble had genuinely been having a great time all night doing what normal teens his age were supposed to do. He wondered what it would have been like to still be in school and hanging around Haven and Mila for a while even had him thinking about at least getting his GED. He may have been too late for high school but college was still an option. O'shea would have a fit if he found out about his son's thoughts but Haven assured him that she had his back if he decided to go through with it. While Haven was thinking about the fakes that invaded her space, Trouble was thinking about what he had to get done. The day he decided to give his life back to God in her closet, Trouble never got the chance to sit down and talk to her.

The sounds of Sza blared through the speakers inside of the ballroom as Haven danced up on Trouble. Never in a million years would she have ever felt comfortable enough to behave the way that she now was. He helped her to find that confidence that she lacked and no one taught her. Trouble told her the truth about everything and she felt obligated to do the same.

Turning around Haven looked up into Trouble's face and smiled. He was so handsome to her and every time she was around him her heart fluttered. They had yet to really make things official with words but their actions showed otherwise.

"Um can we go somewhere and talk right fast?" Haven asked him.

"Yeah let's go. I need to talk to you too," he revealed.

Grabbing her hand they walked out of the crowded room but not before Trouble made eye contact with Fangas. Nodding his head he already knew that the time was near but Trouble did something that he hadn't done in years.

He prayed.

Trouble prayed that what he had to say wouldn't cause her to hate him. He had been battling all night with himself about what to do and her wanting to talk to him was the perfect opportunity.

The two of them stood a little ways down from the ballroom where it wasn't as loud. Haven could hear her heart beating in her ears and she wondered if Trouble could hear it.

"You want me to go first?" he asked her.

Smiling she shook her head no. If he was to go first she would probably chicken out depending on what he told her. She needed to get her thoughts out and let the cards fall where they may.

"First, I want to thank you," she started.

"For what?"

"For coming into my life and entering my heart. I mean I know that we are young and some would say that what I'm feeling would be because of me having daddy issues," she chuckled softly.

"I don't think that."

"Thanks because that couldn't be further from the truth. I mean yeah, I have issues with Daddy but that's not why I feel the way that I do about you. Some of my actions have been to kind of get back at him though. But I feel like you genuinely get me and want the best for me. The way you have helped me to pull out my inner strength I can't thank you enough," she confessed.

"I can't take credit for that Hay. I know I'm not into the church like that but I do know that God is the only one that can help you tap into that strength. He just used me as a vessel I guess. While I was helping you, you were helping me too. I'm starting to look at things differently than before."

Sadness began to set in with the mention of God. Lately it felt like she was falling further away from God and Trouble was drawing nearer. While she was rebelling against her father because of the secrets that he had yet to reveal, she was indulging in activities that she knew was frowned upon. One activity in particular was the reason that she needed to talk to him.

"I need to tell you something else."

"I'm listening."

Trouble didn't know what she was about to say but he was nervous.

"I'm pregnant," she whispered with tears in her eyes.

"Huh? Wait what?" he asked. Trouble felt like his stomach and his heart had just dropped to the bottom of his feet and all of the air in his body had been sucked from it.

The whole time he had been holding her hand but after her revelation he dropped it and backed up against the wall. No logical thought would form in his mind and he didn't know what to say. What she had just told him confirmed what he had been thinking as he thought back to the night that everything happened.

Haven walked Trouble up the stairs and back to her room. The effects of the weed and Mila's drink had Haven feeling some type of way. All of the many lessons that she had been taught about saving herself for marriage were thrown out the window. She wanted Trouble in a way that she never imagined.

Breaking the kiss Trouble paused.

"Wait Haven. We don't have to do this, he said shocking himself. He didn't sleep around on the regular but when he saw something he wanted and it was thrown at him he partook. Haven was different. The girls and grown women that he had been with in the past weren't

worthy of his respect because they rarely respected themselves. This time he had come across someone that he wanted to respect because she deserved it.

"Please Asa," Haven begged.

The way she looked in his eyes and called him by his government name broke him down. One thing led to another that night and they crossed a line that couldn't be undone. The moment their bodies connected there was no going back, not that either of them wanted to. Haven had been taught for as long as she could remember how important it was to remain abstinent until married. That her body was only supposed to be for her husband and him only.

The whole night and half of the next day had been spent inside of her bedroom with not one care or thought about her daddy coming home. He never came back early anyway.

"Asa?"

Haven watched the expression on his face change so many times she was scared of what he was going to say when he finally found the words to speak. Never in a million years did she think she would be an unwed teenage mother. God had to have been fuming with her because she knew better but what was she to do? It was the wakeup call that she needed to get back on track. The careless decisions that she made thinking she would get her father's attention had backfired in the worst way.

"How do you know? How far along are you? Damn man!" Trouble rambled off.

As much as Haven wanted to reach out to him she was scared. Was he mad? Did he believe it was his or did he think she was one of those girls that went around trapping men with babies for money. That wasn't her and she prayed that he knew that.

"I found out yesterday. Mila bought me a test because I was just feeling off. I thought maybe it was because my cycle was soon to come but then I realized that I hadn't had it. This is your baby Asa," Haven rushed out.

The last thing that Trouble was thinking was that the baby wasn't his. He knew for a fact that it was. They had been so caught up in the moment that he didn't even bother to protect either of them and that was what he was kicking himself in the behind for. He made sure to get tested regularly because he was sexually active but not because he was being reckless. He taught himself to always wear protection but he could never be too careful. This was the only time since he lost his virginity at the age of thirteen, that he had slipped up.

"I don't believe in abortions," Haven almost whispered but Trouble heard her loud and clear.

Right before the gunshots rang out.

Thinking as quickly as he could, Trouble pulled Haven into the opposite direction of where the shots were sounding off. To him it sounded like they were already in the ballroom and that meant that whoever was in there busting off were either already in there or had entered through the back door. Trouble's gut was telling him that his father had taken matters into his own hands but he was a step ahead. For some time, he had been planning what he was going to do without telling anyone but one person. Now that he knew that Haven was carrying his child he had to make sure she was good.

"Haven look at me," Trouble said before peeping around the corner. People were starting to run out of the double doors in the opposite direction of where they stood.

Haven was shaking so bad that it was hard for him to get her attention.

"Haven! Listen to me. There is a black Impala parked on the parking deck on the second floor. As soon as you come out of the stairway it's right beside the stairs. Take these keys and push the home button on the GPS. The tank is full and when you get there my Granna will be waiting. She'll explain everything."

"I..I..can't Asa," she began before he cut her off with a kiss and stuffed the keys in her hand.

"Yes you can. Go and don't stop! Now!" he told her.

Haven was in shock but as soon as she saw him reach behind his back and revealed the gun that was hidden in his waistband, she knew that it was time to go. Trouble looked back at her one last time before running back towards the ballroom. Kicking her heels off she went in the opposite direction and through the door that led to the stairs. The whole time she prayed that she made it to the car unnoticed.

As soon as she got into the car, she was glad that it was backed up into the parking space and all she had to do was drive. Haven's hands were shaking and her heart was pounding through her chest as she drove normally around the parking deck towards the entrance. The last thing she wanted was to draw attention to herself.

Hitting the home button on the GPS she saw that she had an hour drive ahead of her. She didn't know anyone in the city that she was headed to but she trusted that God would keep her safe. Her phone was left inside of the ballroom with Mila so she couldn't call her daddy.

Mila!

"God please let her be ok," Haven prayed aloud. Her adrenaline had been pumping so much and her thoughts on protecting herself and her baby, that she didn't even think about Mila. Her heart wanted her to turn around but just as soon as the thought came a sense of peace came over her body.

Praying one last time for her best friend, classmates, and now her child's father, Haven jumped on the highway and breathed out a sigh of relief. She had seen too many movies and read too many books where people didn't pay attention to their surroundings and were being followed. Looking into the rearview mirror and seeing no one behind her let her know that she was protected by grace and would live to see another day.

Back at the hotel Trouble stood outside of the doors with his gun planted firmly in his hands. The gunshots had ceased and he quickly peeped his head inside. All he could see were bodies everywhere but he couldn't make out who was who.

"Aye we gotta go bro!" Fangas yelled when he noticed Trouble at the entrance. He was standing at the far end of the room holding the door open.

Rushing through the crowd they heard the sirens getting closer and knew that if they didn't hurry they wouldn't make it out alive or as free men. There was a truck that was waiting on them with the door open as they rushed inside and it pulled off.

"Yo what was that about?" Trouble asked although he felt like he knew.

"Your old man felt like you were taking too long to do what he needed so he set his plan in motion," Fangas informed him nonchalantly.

"I told him that I had it covered," Trouble responded.

"Please let me go," they heard from behind them.

Trouble looked behind him and noticed someone in the backseat with a bag over their head.

"Who is that?" Trouble asked.

"Since you didn't grab old girl like we told you we did it ourselves. Fangas told us what she looked like.

It took everything in Trouble's power to not show his emotions when he noticed Fangas wasn't looking at him. That alone was all that he needed for his suspicions to be confirmed. Instead of revealing his hand, Trouble sat back and played his part. Silently he prayed that Haven had gotten to the safe spot and was good. It would take a while for them to be able to reconnect because once it was revealed that they had the wrong girl, Trouble's every move would be clocked. The last thing that he wanted to happen was for his Granna and Haven to be harmed before he could eliminate the one person that pulled all of the strings. His father O'shea, better known as the infamous Chop.

~*10*~

"Make sure that nobody pays back wrong for wrong..."

1 Thessalonians 5:15

December 24.1999

    O'shea "Chop" Thomas sat across the street looking up at the building where he knew his next victim was. Sitting beside him and in the back of the car were three of his most trustworthy hittas waiting on him to give them the signal. Smoke filled the car as they puffed on some of Jamaica's strongest ganga.

    People were coming and going getting their last minute holiday shopping done. Smiles covered their faces showing the joy they felt when the only thing that Chop felt was rage. Initially he was just going to take the life of the person that stole from him but that was too easy. Changing his mind at the last minute he had an even better idea.

    Almost an hour later the main door to the building opened and out walked Keys. At one point in time the two men had been cool. Both respecting the other and getting money. Although they were both in the same business of selling drugs they never stepped onto each other's territory. That was until Keys let greed get the best of him and decided he wanted it all. Chop never suspected that he was involved until one of his workers came up off the information.

Chop had no idea that someone within his organization would go against him. Not only was everybody eating just as good as he was but they also knew that he was ruthless when he was crossed. The name Chop didn't come because he was a fan of pork chops but from the fact that he was quick to chop off body parts of his victims. If a body came up with missing limbs or a head ten times out of ten it was him who had done it.

Keys jumped into the car and headed in the opposite direction from where Chop was parked. He already knew where Keys was heading and that soon he would be heading back to his apartment and trying to skip town with his family.

"Let's get it."

That was all that needed to be said before everyone filed out of the car. No masks, no gloves, and weapons clearly visible they made their way inside. Chop wasn't worried about anyone snitching because they wouldn't live to testify. Too many government officials and law enforcement were on his payroll.

Silence filled the stairway. There was no need to talk any longer because instructions were given weeks ago. It had been six months since Keys had robbed him but Chop was a patient man when it came to carrying out a plan. He knew that Keys would be on high alert and just like he had known, Keys moved out of his house soon after. It didn't take long at all for Chop to find out his location and when he did he still opted not to move until the time was right.

Boom!

Sly kicked the door down and granted them access. Entering last, Chop looked around and became enraged even more. The living space was decorated with expensive items and he knew that no one could have decorated it that nicely but one person.

Kenya. She had been his for as long as he could remember but only in his mind. He tried everything to get the cutie from Queens on his roster but she wasn't having it. Time and time again she shattered his ego by telling him that she wasn't interested in being a queen pin. That wasn't the part that made him mad but the fact that she ended up with the man he loathed. For someone that wasn't interested in being a so called queen pin she wore the crown proudly and stood by her king. There had been *times that she would bust her gun just as loud as Keys and that was the sexiest thing to Chop ever.*

Pop! Pop! Pop!

Gunshots rang out followed by a scream and what sounded like a body dropping. Chop stood in the middle of the apartment like he was bulletproof and one of the bullets couldn't strike him through the wall. He moved carefree towards the back and just as he got to the bedroom door the shots ended and he heard moaning.

Gun still gripped as tightly as she could hold it, Chop saw her lift her head towards the movement in her room. His shadow covered her the moment her vision started to go.

"Keys thought it was ok to steal from me?" Chop asked rhetorically.

Kenya knew that voice and knew it well. Satan himself stood above her with the barrel of his gun trained on her and she wearily returned the gesture with her own gun.

"Still a fighter I see."

With everything in her, Kenya spit on his shoes.

The ultimate form of disrespect.

That millisecond of losing focus because she was angry gave him just what he needed in order to release the bullet that put Kenya out of her misery.

"And still disrespectful too."

With those final words, he stepped back and looked at the bodies around him smiling. He wasn't worried about the police showing up right away because he had most of them on his payroll. He couldn't help but to smile knowing that the woman he had always wanted by his side was just as gutter as he was. She had taken out all four of the men that he had run up in her and her man's apartment with.

Reaching behind him he pulled out his favorite machete that he carried with him and swiftly cut off the hand that held the five carat engagement ring.

"Save a seat in hell for Chop beautiful."

With that Chop wiped off the machete with the blanket that was disheveled on the bed and exited alone. It would only be a matter of time before Keys would meet the same fate as Kenya and they could be together in death.

***

Fifteen minutes after Keys left his fiancé and child he was pulling up to one of his trap houses. Something was off because there was no one outside. That wasn't normal. Usually the only time the street looked like a ghost town was when something had jumped off and they didn't want to be questioned by police or threatened by whoever committed the crime.

It wasn't too late in the evening but it was dark enough for Keys to tell that the lights to his main trap were off. Pulling out his gun he decided to walk around to the back of the house and enter. The moment he got there and saw the back door left wide open he understood the silence of the neighborhood.

Keys picked up his pace and removed the safety. There was no way for him to know if someone was still inside or not so he had to be on point. At any given time there was always three people working in the spot. One was counting money, the other cooking up the dope, and one that was separating the final product for distribution. All three of his workers lay with their body parts scattered around them and that was all Keys needed to see to know who had done it.

With panic setting in, Keys turned on his heels without checking the rest of the house. He already knew that all of his product and money was gone but what worried him even more than that was knowing that if Chop was responsible he needed to get his girl and daughter out of the city.

Going against his better judgement right after he robbed Chop, Keys knew that he should have left the state but he couldn't. At least not right away. There was money that needed to be made before he could do so. When the time was right he would leave but not a minute sooner. His gut was telling him that it was time to go and that was just what he planned to do.

Keys ran all lights and stop signs trying to get back home. There was no way to stop and warn Kenya but he knew his girl was always strapped. She shot first and would ask questions never. He just didn't want her to be caught off guard and with his baby girl inside. No police cars were in front of his building when he got there and that gave him a little bit of relief. Maybe he had gotten there in time to get them out. That theory was debunked as soon as he got up the last step and saw his door laying in the hallway.

Letting out a plethora of curse words, Keys headed straight to his bedroom. His heart was crushed and his lungs felt like they were suffocating in his chest. Chop's men were sprawled out riddled with bullets and Kenya was lifeless on the floor. Her left hand was missing and if Keys didn't know who was responsible before he did then.

His baby!

Where was his baby? He looked around to the spot where he last saw her before he left and it was empty. Moving quickly through the room he searched all under and around the bed. He could only see red as he thought about something happening to his child. Just as he was about to leave out of the room and search the rest of the apartment he heard a whimper along with sirens in the distance.

"Where are you baby?" Keys searched frantically until he heard the noise again. Immediately his eyes landed on the dresser drawer that was slightly opened and ran over to it.

Quickly he prayed when he saw the blood that ran down the front of the dresser. If his daughter was hurt he would be painting all five boroughs red until he found Chop and ended his life. The moment he looked inside and grabbed his baby he moved the blanket gently just in case she was injured. When he saw that the blood didn't belong to her he wasted no time getting out of there.

Cradled in his arms his daughter cooed and he thanked God for keeping her safe. With all of the bullets that were sprayed throughout the room it was a miracle that not one had hit her. The blood that he had seen was more than likely from the men that Kenya had shot. He didn't know why the loud sounds of the shots didn't cause her to scream out but he was thankful that she didn't. If she did she may not have been alive to see another day. Given the fact that she was, he had to change his plans of wreaking havoc in order to protect Haven.

~11~

"Their malice may be concealed by deception, but their wickedness will be exposed in the assembly."

Proverbs 26:26

Tears filled Hosea's eyes as he stood behind the pulpit and looked down on the casket that was in front of the church. Some may have thought he was crying because of the funeral he was officiating but that couldn't be any further from the truth. He couldn't see the body that had found it to be its final resting bed because of the top that was open. He looked out into the congregation at a sea of mixed emotions. There were people that looked uninterested, some looked relieved, but most looked genuinely sad.

"Sister Brianna was a wonderful and sweet soul. She was dedicated to serving the Lord with all of her heart and I know that the angels are rejoicing about her homecoming," he spoke.

Thoughts of Haven crossed his mind continuously and he was so sick on the inside not knowing where she was. The last time that he had seen her over a week ago, she was dressed beautifully and heading off to her senior prom. Never in a million years would he have thought that would be the last time that he saw her. He didn't know where to even begin looking and the police weren't much help. Even Asa was unable to give him any information and the last time he saw her was before he went to the bathroom that night.

Asa let him know that they were all having a good time and dancing and then he excused himself before leaving the ballroom. Before he had the chance to return there was a shootout and he tried his best to find her but was unable to. Police even thought they had found her a day later but the body of the young girl wasn't Haven. It was one of her classmates who had vaguely resembled her and had on a dress that was similar to the one Hosea had told them she was wearing. He didn't know who the girl's parents were but his heart had gone out to them for their loss.

For some reason Hosea didn't believe Asa. It wasn't his spirit telling him anything but it was his street knowledge that led him to believe it. How and why Asa would do something to her was beyond him but stranger things have happened. Getting his thoughts focused on the task at hand, Hosea cleared his throat and continued on with the eulogy.

"Sister Brianna's presence will forever be missed but her impact on the children in the children's ministry as well as her support of the other auxiliaries that she participated in will live on for years to come.

At this time if you would like to say a few words about the dearly departed, we ask that you only take about a minute to two minutes to share. I know we all loved her and want to share so many good memories of her."

One at a time people stood and made their way to the middle aisle to wait their turn. A few couldn't even finish because of the overwhelming feeling that took over. Hosea watched as Brianna's mother had to be carried to the back where the nurse's office was because she had cried so hard she passed out.

Just as the last person had finished speaking the doors to the back of the church opened and a sea of police officers, detectives, and federal agents swarm inside. They all went in different directions and from the monitor that was positioned under the pulpit Hosea saw that they were going straight for his office. Living the life that he did he felt like he could never be too safe and had installed a stated of the art security system with monitors throughout the building. He never wanted to be caught up while preaching by an enemy that was out to get him. His thoughts were so focused on Haven that he hadn't looked at the monitor not once.

Words had gotten stuck in his throat as he watched his office cam and saw an agent head straight for the secret door that led to his trap room. He was bothered by the fact that all of the drugs, guns, and money that was hidden in there would be found and he would no doubt be sent to jail, but what disturbed him even more was how they knew exactly where to go.

The only other person outside of he and Shaunie that knew about what was hid behind his bookcase was laying in the white casket that was covered in royal blue flowers. It reminded him of that episode of *Power* where the gun that was planted by Sandoval was found in order to arrest Ghost. The only difference was that no one planted evidence that didn't belong to Hosea. Everything in that room was his and there was nothing that he could do about it.

"Hosea Reynolds?" a Hispanic detective questioned him.

"Yes. Pastor Hosea Reynolds and we are in the middle of a homegoing service for one of our members. Can whatever you need be done at a later time? The family and friends of Sister Stevens deserve to grieve and say goodbye to their loved one."

"You mean the loved one that you murdered?" she asked matter-of-factly followed by a sea of gasps.

"I-I'm not sure what you are talking about," he stuttered. Almost instantly beads of sweat began to appear on his forehead and the bridge of his nose. The tie around his neck seemed to get tighter and caused him to raise his hand in order to loosen it some.

"We have a confession from a Chinirika Stanbury."

A confused expression was plastered to Hosea's face but before he could ask who that person was or tell them he had no idea of who that was, the side door leading from the sanctuary to the hallway that led to his office opened. Officer after officer walked in carrying the evidence that he had yet to have moved and his heart sank. The people that were there to celebrate a life were now being exposed to the real person that he was. To them he had been Pastor Hosea Reynolds for the last fifteen years but now he would have his identity revealed as Hosea "Keys" Reynolds.

"What are you doing?" a woman yelled out. She was sitting on the pew in the front row so he assumed she was a relative of Brianna. As soon as the detective touched the bottom of the casket and released the latch to the bottom half she was up out of her seat and was being restrained by one of the boys in blue.

Hosea watched with his eyes bucked out because he knew exactly what they were going for. He didn't have her body disposed of after he ordered the hit on her the day she found out his secret because he was going to need her. Had he not decided to have a funeral he wouldn't have been able to use her casket and the hearse out front to transport the drugs that were now being pulled from the lining in the box.

"Mercy God!"

"Jesus be a fence!"

"God I rebuke this false prophet!"

People in the church began to call out. They had never seen anything like what was going on in front of them in real life. The closest they would ever get to something of that magnitude would be in movies. Cell phones were coming out and all of social media was privy to the what was going on inside. It didn't take long for local news outlets to begin pouring in as Hosea was handcuffed.

"I don't know what is going on! This stuff isn't mine," he yelled.

"Chile and he still lying in the house of God," Mother Maxine scoffed and shook her head.

"It's a special place in hell for people like you," someone else said.

"Who is Chinirika Stanbury?" he asked wanting to know the person that had so much info on him and his activities.

"That would be me," a voice said.

Hosea turned his head in the direction of the familiar voice and his suspicions were confirmed.

"Shaunie?"

~12~

"When I said, 'My foot is slipping,' your unfailing love, Lord, supported me."

Psalm 94:18

Haven was an emotional wreck. The events of the past week were starting to take their toll on her. There was only so much strength in the Lord that she had left and if something didn't change soon she was sure she would break down completely.

Rubbing her stomach gently there was no baby bump but that didn't stop her from knowing there was a life growing in there. No matter how sinful the act of premarital sex was she knew that her baby was a blessing. Time and time again after that night with Trouble she had repented daily. Not just for what happened but for wanting it to happen again. It was true, once you opened your spirit up to anything, good or bad, it had the opportunity to attach itself to your life. Thoughts would be consumed by it and it would be a battle that some died trying to win.

The night of her prom after everything went down and she arrived at her destination she had been praying nonstop. Not only was she constantly in God's face so was Trouble's grandma on her behalf. Granna was such a sweet woman and had it not been for her Haven wouldn't have been able to get through the days although it was now getting more difficult. Before she could let the tears drop there was a knock at the bedroom door.

"Sweetie it's me. Can I come in?" Granna asked from the other side of the door.

"Yes ma'am," Haven replied just above a whisper.

Granna entered the room and smiled at Haven. The night that the young girl arrived at her front door she was already prepared for her arrival. Her grandbaby Asa had already brought clothes and personal necessities that Haven would need for the time that she was there. Because he didn't know how long she would need to be there he made sure to leave extra money for the both of them. Granna insisted that she would make sure that Haven would have everything she needed but he wasn't trying to hear that. It was the first time that she had seen or heard her grandbaby taking any little girl serious and she approved one hundred percent.

What she was on the fence about was the baby that she found out would be a part of their young lives in a few short months. She had no idea how things would play out and she was not only nervous for them but scared as well. O'shea was not wrapped too tight and he wouldn't stop until he wreaked havoc on the people that he felt wronged him and without a doubt Asa going against him was a no no.

"Are you alright baby?" Granna asked coming further into the room.

Haven watched the beautiful older lady and wondered what her own grandmother would have been like. She only remembered her a little bit because just like her mother she was young when Mama Ruby passed away. Granna reminded Haven of her grandmother because she was so soft spoken and loving but she looked like if anything went left she would pop off if needed. That thought alone caused Haven to wear a slight smile as the woman sat beside her.

Ethel Green, or Granna as she was affectionately called, was a tall woman. She had long gray hair that came to the middle of her back. Her front bang was twisted around a single pink sponge roller. Haven didn't even know that they still sold those kind of rollers anymore and they probably didn't considering the one she was wearing looked very worn out. Granna's skin was a flawless coffee with cream complexion and there wasn't a wrinkle in sight except for the crow's feet around her eyes. Other than that no one could tell that she was going on seventy years old.

"Not good Granna. I mean given all of the circumstances of me being here and everything," she spoke honestly.

"I understand baby but I trust God in this all. I'm thankful the life of you and that precious little one was spared that night. It could have been so much worse."

"You're right I guess."

The two of them sat silently for a few moments before Haven spoke again.

"Have you heard from Asa?"

Shaking her head no was all that Granna could do. If she had opted to use words she was sure that she would break out into tears and she didn't want Haven to be worried about consoling her. She had called Asa so many times on the number that he gave her to call but he had yet to answer or return any of her calls. Fear wanted to set in but Granna knew that she served a mighty God. Besides when her daughter was murdered, instantly she felt it. Just like when both of her parents passed away she knew then too. It was like an invisible spear shot her right in the heart causing more pain than she had ever felt in her life. Each time after that first time she knew exactly what it meant when her heart began to hurt.

"I cooked. Let's go get you and my little princess something to eat," Granna told her while patting Haven's thigh.

"How do you know it's a girl?" Haven wanted a little girl so that she could be the mother that she missed out on having but she would just be happy if the baby was healthy. Seventeen years old and not even a graduate of high school and there she was about to have a baby without a husband.

"Oh I just have my gut feeling that's all."

Getting up, Haven followed Granna to the front of the house and into the kitchen. Immediately the smell of oxtails, rice and beans, cabbage, and fried plantain hit her nose. The sight of the warm cocoa bread that sat in the middle of the counter had Haven's mouthwatering. If there was anything that Haven loved more than God and her father it was Jamaican food. She could eat it every day if she had the opportunity to and would never get tired of it.

"I love Jamaican food Granna!" Haven said excitedly.

"Asa told me. He said that every time he was with you that's all you wanted to eat. He even told me that he was going to take you to Jamaica one day so that you could get the full experience." Hearing that Asa talked about her so much and remembered the small things caused Haven to smile from ear to ear.

Granna finished making their plates and handed Haven hers before grabbing two Jamaican sodas from the refrigerator and leading them into the living room. Trouble had really gone all out and gotten everything that he thought she would like and want. She couldn't wait to see him so that she could throw her arms around him and thank him.

"Granna what you know about this?" Haven asked surprised when she saw her land on *Vh1's Love and Hip Hop Atlanta.*

"Girl I love me some Steebie," she laughed referring to the producer Stevie J.

"Unt uh Granna. Let me find out you trying to be a cougar," Haven laughed.

"Baby listen, if he ever crossed my path I could make him forget about that so called Puerto Rican princess and Molly the maid. Shole will now."

Haven almost choked on the rice that she had just stuffed in her mouth. Tears were falling from her eyes as she laughed like she hadn't laughed in a long time.

"Lord you are a mess Granna!"

Shrugging her shoulders like she didn't know what Haven was talking about had her laughing even more because she was so serious. No matter what happened with her and Asa, she was going to make sure that she stayed in contact with Granna. That old woman was funny, could cast out the meanest demon, genuinely loved people, and most importantly cooked the best Jamaican food hands down!

The two of them watched a few episodes while they ate and when they were done Haven could feel sleep trying to overtake her.

"Lord Granna that was so good."

"I'm glad you enjoyed it sweetie."

"Did I?"

Haven was just about to prop her feet up on the couch and throw the blanket that was over the back of the couch across her body when the doorbell rang. It was as if time stood still for them both. Haven was sure that whoever on the other side of the door could hear her heart beating because it was just that loud. Even Granna was nervous because she didn't know who it was. Trouble had made sure to tell her that the only time she was to open the door was when he called her to tell her that someone would be by. If he didn't she was to never open it under any circumstance. The moment Haven arrived she was informed of the same thing.

"Granna it's me!" they heard Trouble call out.

Granna thought Haven should have been named Flo Jo because of how fast she sprinted from the couch and over to the door. Swinging it open she had tears in her eyes and a smile on her lips when she saw him standing there. Just like she had yearned to do since the last time she saw him, her arms flew around his neck as she pulled him inside.

"You ok?" he asked her. Hearing his voice broke her down but all she could do was nod her head and cry.

Was it a sin for her to miss and need someone so bad that it hurt? If so she would just have to repent once again because that was exactly the feeling that overtook her.

"Hey my baby. I've been worried sick about you," Granna told Trouble. Haven finally stepped off to the side to allow her to wrap his tall frame in her arms.

"I know Granna and I'm sorry. I just had to be careful. Are y'all ok?"

"Just worried about you that's all."

"How are you feeling?" he asked Haven. He was so glad that he could finally be in her presence again. Trouble never imagined yearning for a girl the way that he yearned for Haven. Not sexually but just because she was who she was. Sex was the last thing on his mind because he knew that one action had caused something to happen that neither of them were ready for but now they had made their beds. It was time to man up and lie in it.

"Better now that you're here and we know you're alright. Where have you been? What's going on? Have you seen my daddy?" Haven rattled off question after question.

"That's what I came to talk to you about," he told her somberly.

The look in his eyes and how he squeezed her hand let her know that it was serious and the food that she had just enjoyed was threatening to return to the surface. Her nerves were jumping and her breathing was becoming rapid at the thought of what he had to tell her. She didn't even know what it was yet and she was a mess.

"Let's go sit down," Granna instructed. Before she followed them she made sure to look outside and check to make sure that nothing looked out of the ordinary and no one had followed her grandson. She couldn't be too sure and unlike last time she was going to be prepared that time.

Locking the door, she made sure everything was secure before she walked into the living room. Just as she came around the corner Haven let out a blood curdling scream and had it not been for Trouble she would have hit the floor. He held her tightly with both of their eyes trained on the tv. Following their eyes, Granna's attention was trained on the breaking news report and she gasped. There being led out of a church was Haven's father in handcuffs with the headline of the report under him on the screen.

Breaking News: Prominent Pastor Pushed Drugs Through the House of God.

What terrified her more than a person disrespecting the house of the Lord the way that Haven's father had was the fact that the news man turned the camera and caught a glimpse of O'shea standing there with a murderous look in his eyes.

Closing her own, Granna prayed silently that God covered them all. The gates of hell were certainly open and Satan himself was about to start a war that only God and His angels could keep them protected from.

~13~

"The end of a matter is better than its beginning, and patience is better than pride." Ecclesiastes 7:8

Trouble wanted so bad to get to his grandmother and Haven but he knew that he had to be patient. Not only did their lives depend on it so did his. He knew that if he moved too soon and word got back to his father there would be hell to pay. That was just something that he wasn't willing to risk. Granna had been blowing up the prepaid phone that he had gotten just for her to contact him but things had been so hectic that he couldn't chance answering her and someone overhearing his conversation.

The night of the shootout was still fresh in his mind and just like Trouble thought his father was behind it. He felt like Trouble was moving too slow on what needed to be done so he took it upon himself to get things done with the help of Fangas. Trouble always had a feeling that his so called friend was a snake but there was a part of him that wanted to disregard it. There was that spirit of discernment that Granna always talked about that seemed to ring off like an alarm the first time they met but he never paid attention to it until recently. It was because of that he was able to stay ten steps ahead of his father and the plan that he set. Especially once he heard the one thing that put fire under his behind to make a move.

O'shea or Chop as the streets called him had violated one of his many rules of not letting everyone in your business. Because Fangas was eager to prove his loyalty to Chop he had let him in on a little too much information. Information that had changed everything for Trouble.

"Once I come through for Chop, OG ain't gonna be able to do nothing but put me in my rightful place," *Fangas said through a cloud of smoke. The blunt that he was smoking was laced with the best weed mixed with heroine that he had ever smoked and it was causing him to run his mouth like he had diarrhea.*

Trouble had been running late to the trap house for pick up because he had just finished moving Granna into her new house. The one that his father had no idea about. He had been feeling like something was going to hit the fan and to be on the safe side he needed to make sure that she was in a safe place that no one could find her.

"Man what makes you think Chop gonna put you in front of his son?" Sleeze asked taking the blunt from

between Fangas long fingers. He would never say it out loud but Sleeze didn't trust Fangas or Chop. He was just working to make money for his family and one day he felt he would have enough money to move away and start a new life. Although his name came from how grimey he could be in the streets he knew that lifestyle wasn't meant for him. But in the meantime and in between time he would do what he had to for his family.

"Bruh trust me Asa not 'bout this life," he laughed calling Trouble by his birth name.

"Looks like to me he been holding his own."

"That nigga ain't making no real moves. If it wasn't for me he would have never bumped into that fat ass girl."

Sleeze's eyes got big just as Trouble's interest was piqued. He was about to walk into the back room until he heard Haven's name. His hand dropped form the doorknob like it was a hot piece of coal that would burn a hole through it if he had touched it.

"What you mean?"

"I been knew that Chop was gone tell us to get at ole girl. He told me his plan first and I had been watching her for a little bit. You know seeing who she hung with and what she was about."

"Uh huh."

"So when I saw her I already knew she was gone be a hard one but her little friend was easier. The day we ran into them was just by chance and I couldn't let it pass so I told Trouble to pull over like I wanted to holla. When he did I asked him to keep Thunder Thighs occupied while I got in her friend's head."

"Why you keep calling that girl names man?"

"Shoot I ain't lying!" Fangas laughed. Trouble on the other side of the door found nothing funny though. He was just about to walk in when something else stopped him.

Fangas went on to explain in detail the reason that Haven was so important. From her father being one of the biggest drug dealers in Queens and him robbing Chop to his own father being the one to kill Haven's mother. That piece of information made Trouble realize that he and Haven really did have a lot in common. They both had fathers that lied to them their whole lives and was responsible for both of their mother's deaths.

"Chop is cold blooded though. Anytime you can kill your kids mother on the strength of her leaving you 'cause she got tired of the beatings you know a nigga heartless. Then on top of that you start smashing the broad that snitched on her best friend's whereabouts."

"Chinirika?" Sleeze choked out. That was something that he didn't see coming and it caused him to inhale too much weed smoke.

"Light weight," Fangas laughed and snatched the blunt back.

That was all that Trouble could take hearing. The anger that rose in him learning that his mother's death came at the hands of the man that helped create him was something that he just couldn't take. Then on top of that Chinirika was involved. He knew that he had never liked her and for good reason too.

Backing out of the house he was glad that the workers were slacking and not in place like they should have been. No one would know that he was there and that he had heard everything. Well almost everything. He still didn't know the plan that Chop had for Haven but given all that he had heard he knew that when it was all said and done her blood would be on his hands.

Trouble had made it up in his head as he drove back towards Granna's house, that if he had anything to do with it and God was really with him he was going to make sure that Haven was protected. Or he would die trying.

***

Fangas rambled on and on about how he couldn't believe that he had gotten the wrong girl kidnapped at the prom. There was so much chaos in the large room and bullets flying everywhere that he really couldn't see much. The last place that he had seen Haven she was sitting in the spot that he grabbed the girl that was hiding under the table.

Trouble just sat there with his best mean mug on and got ready to play the role of the century. Since Fangas wanted to be sneaky and backstabbing it was only a matter of time before his fate was handed to him. He was in a pure panic mode because the plan that he thought was fool proof had been unraveled and Chop was on the war path.

"What the hell happened?!" Chop roared. He entered the warehouse with murder on his mind and a Glock in his hand. Somebody was going to pay for the mess up but no one knew who.

Pow!

Chop sent one single bullet between the eyes of the girl that was kidnapped and put her out of her misery. As bad as Trouble felt for her because she was innocent he didn't let it show on his face. He knew that Chop would be looking for anything that showed Trouble wasn't feeling what was going down and as soon as he saw it his own life would be taken.

Trouble looked from the girl sprawled out on the floor in a dress that resembled the one Haven had on and then straight up into the eyes of his father.

Nothing.

No remorse. No fear. Not a care in the world. Those were the things that Trouble showed Chop causing him to turn his attention to Fangas.

"I asked a question," Chop told him.

"I had everything planned out. I saw where ole girl was sitting at and then I texted Sleeze to let him know it was a go. The crew came in with guns blazing and I went for her. I knew that she couldn't have gotten far because I was already close to where she was sitting. I grabbed her and threw the bag over her head. How was I to know that some of those school boys was strapped and started bussin' back?"

It was true. A few of the boys that went to Haven's school was deep in the streets and as soon and bullets began to fly they were returning fire of their own. After Trouble got Haven out of the building and rushed back into the room he saw them hiding behind the overturned buffet. Trouble made it out of the back door just in time to hop in the van and speed away.

"And where were you?" Chop directed the question to Trouble.

"I was in the lobby. A little cutie was trying to take me upstairs to her room when the shots popped off. By the time I ran back to the ballroom I saw Fangas leaving out the door with the girl and I ran behind him. From where I was it looked like he already had ole girl so I jumped in the ride. I didn't know that it wasn't her until we got here in the light," Trouble explained with a straight face and a convincing recount of what happened.

Pow!

Fanga's body dropped to the ground and Trouble didn't even flinch. He couldn't feel bad about what Chop did because Fangas was disloyal and he knew what came with that lifestyle. The one that he wanted to live so bad and Trouble never wanted to be a part of had finally caught up to him.

"Where's your grandmother?" Chop asked out of the blue. The two of them along with a few of the other members of the crew were standing around like there weren't two dead bodies at their feet.

"I guess at home," Trouble replied. His brows were furrowed like he was wondering why he was being asked where she was at such a random time.

"Give me your phone," Chop ordered.

Trouble did everything in his power not to smirk because he knew what Chop was looking for but he was confident he wouldn't find it. He watched his father unlock his phone and go straight to the call log and text threads between him and Granna. The last call being a week prior that lasted only for a few minutes just like normal. Then there was a text right before prom. He had sent her a picture of him in his tux before leaving the house and one with both him and Haven together.

Not finding anything that showed that Trouble knew where she was other than the last place that she lived, Chop handed him his phone back and walked off.

"Find the girl," was all Chop said before exiting the room they were in and making it back to his office.

"Want me to follow him?" one of his henchmen named Camo questioned.

"Yeah. Don't stop until I tell you to stop either."

"Gotcha boss."

"If you mess this up you better kiss that fine wife you got and those little snot nosed kids of yours goodbye.

The last time you see them will be before the funeral director lowers them into the ground."

Camo didn't take too kindly to people threatening his family but there was nothing that he could do about it. He knew that it was only a matter of time before someone chopped Chop down from that high horse he was sitting on. He just hoped that they did it soon.

~14~

"Cain said to the Lord, 'My punishment is more than I can bear.'"

Genesis 4:13

Hosea, or Keys as the world now knew him, sat in his cell staring at the wall. He couldn't believe that everything he had worked so hard for was now flushed down the toilet. He already knew that with the amount of drugs and guns that was found inside of the church he was going to be gone for a long time but now he had other charges he was facing. From racketeering, embezzlement, the murders that he was sure the police would find, and impersonating a pastor; he would be lucky if he only got life. That sentence alone would be a blessing.

Going against the code of the streets, Keys decided that talking to the police that were investigating Kenya's murder might prove to be beneficial to him. He needed it to look like he was this upstanding citizen that was making an honest living and wanted to know what happened to the love of his life. He gave them everything that they wanted to hear while omitting one thing. Thinking quickly he decided to blame the incident on a random junkie that hung around the block. Keys told them there were a few occasions resulting in an altercation with the man because he would constantly try and harass Kenya. It started with him begging for money and being the kindhearted person that she was, she always gave it to him. Then it turned into him hitting on her and even following her up the stairs one late night. Keys lied and said that a scuffle happened about a week before her murder and he remembered the man saying that they would get what was coming to them. He didn't take it seriously and blew it off as nothing.

The police later asked who the other men were that were found in the apartment and Keys said that he didn't know. They were too well dressed to be bums on the street so maybe they were family members or something. Not having too much to go on and ruling Keys out as a suspect he was free to leave. Being that it was just another killing of a black person they didn't really try hard to solve the case and it ended up going cold.

At least that was what he was told. The truth of the matter was that Chop had people on his payroll within the police department that had given him a heads up. He could have easily gone and killed Keys before he left town but he had a better plan. If anything Chop was a very patient man and knew that one day he would get the revenge that he so hungrily sought.

While Keys was being escorted out of the church after finding out Shaunie, or Chinirika, had been lying to him and set him up, he stopped dead in his tracks when his eyes landed on the one man that held Keys' life in the palm of his hands. The way Chop walked up to him and gave what looked to be his sincere condolences on Haven's disappearance, it was in that moment that Keys knew his daughter missing wasn't a coincidence. Seventeen years later, Chop had finally gotten to his only child and finished what he had started. It was as that point he knew he would probably never see her again. His many sins had caught up to him and there was nothing that he could do about it.

His sins.

Something that his mother had warned him of for as long as he could remember. Every time he talked to her she was preaching the word to him and telling him that if he didn't take heed to the warnings that God was giving him there would be hell to pay. Time and time again she called him a man of God but time and time again he would blow her off. He didn't care how many times he heard it there was no way that he was going to walk in a so called calling.

Unlike most people who had issues with church people, he didn't use any of those excuses as the reason for him not wanting to be active in church. He just didn't. That was until his grandmother sparked something in him.

When Keys left New York shortly after the shootout in his apartment, he knew that he needed an out. Never in his wildest dreams would he have thought to use the church as his hideout. Ruby though had unknowingly planted the seed in him and he was ready to water it until it was full grown.

"Baby this is God trying to get your attention. It's time to walk into your calling. I know Reverend Martin will love to have you studying under him and maybe one day you can even start your own church," she told him.

As soon as she said that a light bulb went off in his head. Once again he felt that familiar pull at his heart that over the years had become stronger. He knew what it was but he continued to ignore it. On the road to South Carolina that small still voice was heard periodically doing its best to make him rethink things. The death and destruction that he had been a part of for so long was beginning to weigh him down.

I'm still here and I love you.

Trust me.

"You know what Ma? I think you're right. I've been doing my own thing too long and it's time for me to grow up. Now that I have to raise Haven alone I gotta do better if not for myself then especially for her," he said. Keys looked down at his baby girl who was looking back at him with those pretty eyes of hers like she knew he was lying.

"Lord I thank you Father!" Ruby cried out as tears ran down her face.

Keys hated to lie to her but owning a church on his own was the perfect way to cover up his operation. Since everything had been lost back in New York he had to start from the bottom again. It was going to take a little longer than he wanted but he knew it would be worth it. Having large congregation would allow the money to flow in and he could hide everything inside of the Lord's house. There was no way that anyone would suspect a pastor to be trapping out of something that was so sacred.

It was a perfect, foolproof plan to him at the time but now that he was sitting behind bars he thought differently.

"Reynolds!" one of the guards called out to get his attention.

Looking up Keys said nothing. His intense gaze was as cold as ice and as hard as steel. There was no way that he was going to let them intimidate him while he was there. That was the easiest way to let guards and inmates alike know that they could get under an inmate's skin and once they did there would be no peace.

The guard slid an envelope through the bars and before it had the chance to hit the floor he had walked off. Keys got up and walked over to it slowly before picking it up. He turned it over in his hand and saw that there was nothing written on it. Instantly he got a feeling that whatever was inside, was something that he didn't want.

His heart momentarily stopped and his chest got tight as soon as he pulled out the picture of the girl's body that that was laying in the middle of an open field. She had a bag over her head but Keys would know that dress anywhere. It was the same one that he thought his daughter would look stunning in.

Tears fell from his eyes but he didn't care. Knowing that Haven was all alone before her life was taken was something that he couldn't stomach. All because of greed. He had wanted to live a kingpin's lifestyle and was adamant about doing so. He didn't care who or what he had to sacrifice in order to get it but this wasn't what he wanted. Haven was his world but he never showed her just how much. His love for money overshadowed him being the father that she needed. That thought alone caused him to slide down the cinderblock wall and sob loudly not caring at all who heard him.

After all of the years of him preaching lies he was finally forced to live in his truth.

~15~

"Such a person is double minded in all they do."

James 1:8

Chinirika sat beside Chop as they rode home in silence. It had been another long day of them looking around for Trouble. For almost three months they searched for him but were unsuccessful and she was drained. The baby that was on the inside of her was using up all of her energy and she couldn't wait until she no longer had to hide the fact that she was pregnant. She just had to find out a way to let him know without him making her get an abortion or worse, killing her.

There were plenty of times that he told her that he didn't want any more kids and he was standing his ground. That was the reason that she fell for Keys. She had one job and that was to get on the inside and get close enough to him in order to help Chop's plan for destruction. What she didn't plan on was falling for him and ending up carrying his child.

When she walked into the church the very first time and saw Keys standing behind the pulpit she was all in. Back in Queens she knew who he was and that he was getting money but she only had eyes for Chop. After years of being his main woman things between them started changing when she spoke about having babies. He had shut her down before she could even argue her case. Even still she stayed and went harder to prove her loyalty. It felt like it wasn't enough to snitch on her best friend and get her killed. Chop treated her like that was what she was supposed to do.

It didn't take long at all for her to get close to Keys. Her charm, so called expertise in the administrative field, and sex appeal had him sold. In no time, she had found her way into his bed. That just wasn't a part of her job description. She knew that she could never leave Chop, well not willingly. If anything the only way she would be allowed to leave was in death. There was no doubt that if Chop found out what was really going on with Keys before she was ready he would kill the both of them.

Chinirika's plan was to let Keys know what was up and hopefully he would see her loyalty was to him. Before the opportunity presented itself Trouble showed up to the church causing her to have to change plans. As soon as she saw him and their eyes met it was clear Trouble would tell his father the first chance he got.

Instead of giving him time to expose her she immediately called Chop and gave up all of the information that he needed. That way when Trouble spoke to him he would look like he was trying once again to get her out of the picture but Chop wouldn't believe him.

"What you over there thinking about?" Chop interrupted the silence and her thoughts.

At first it looked like they were on the way home until he turned off and headed into a different direction.

"Huh? Oh nothing baby just a little tired. But um, where are we going?" she asked nervously. She tried to calm herself down but her voice was shaking and she hoped that Chop didn't notice.

Instead of responding to her, Chop just glanced at her and gave her a smile but Chinirika wasn't stupid. Behind those pearly white teeth and beautiful golden eyes was a murder plot and she prayed that it wasn't hers.

Chop never trusted Chinirika or any woman for that matter. He knew that if she could sell out her best friend Lisa to him after he was beating her for years just to be down with him then she couldn't be trusted. The two women had been best friends right out the womb and at the first chance of betrayal in order for a come up, Chinirika took it. Because of that she would never be trusted and little did she know he was on to her.

The only woman that he had given his heart to had crushed it and didn't even know it. Kenya was the one that he had always wanted but she never gave him the chance. As fine and as paid as he was any woman would be lucky to get him to call her his own but Kenya wanted no part of him. It was like he had an obsession with her. She was supposed to sit on the throne with him but she chose not to. It was true that women held a certain power within them that had the potential to drive a man crazy and Kenya had done just that. Especially when she ended up with Keys.

The revenge plot that he set out to get over Keys didn't have much to do with him stealing his dope and money but stealing the one thing that Chop wanted in this world and that was Kenya. Of course he could have moved on and let things end when Kenya took her last breath but anger set in even more because she was dead.

Looking over at Chinirika, Chop could see the fear setting in by the way she kept fidgeting in her seat. He smiled inwardly just imagining all of the thoughts that were going through her mind. If she had really paid attention to how he operated all of those years of being in his presence she would have known that he knew of her intimate relationship with her man of the cloth.

Then again, if he had been focused then he would have known about Trouble moving his grandmother. When his local search came up empty handed around the city he immediately thought Trouble may have been with his grandmother. To his surprise when he arrived and saw the house empty he knew that he needed to find him asap and as soon as he did it was a wrap for him. It wasn't like he was important anyway.

"Who lives here?" Chinirika asked doing her best to sound normal. Her hands were shaking and she tried her best to calm her nerves.

"Get out."

Doing as she was told without question she slowly exited the foreign car and extended her hand towards the one he held out to her. The moment their skin connected she knew there was a great possibility that she wouldn't be leaving alive. She wondered if there was a place for someone like her in heaven. Although majority of the time when Keys was in pastor mode he preached a generic message there were times when she picked up the bible on her own. The one scripture that stood out to her the most was first John chapter one and verse nine.

'If we confess our sins, He is faithful and just to forgive us our sins, and to cleanse us from all unrighteousness.'

Chinirika knew that she had committed some of the most heinous sins imaginable and there was no way that God would forgive her. All ten of His commandments had been broken ten times over with others added to it. It was then that she thought about how cliché it must be to God for some people to be in the face of death before they really acknowledged Him. They cried out for forgiveness after years of going against Him but when they were about to leave this earth then they remembered who He was.

Not her. Chinirika wasn't about to be one of those hypocrites in her last moments of life. She would hold her head high in her wrong doing. What good would it do for her to ask for forgiveness and then find out that He didn't really forgive her? She would be in hell anyway so what was the point?

"Baby I would rather live my life like God is real and abide by His teachings and die to find out that He isn't than; to live my life like He isn't and die to find out He is."

Chinirika could hear her mother Kimberly's voice just a clear as day reciting one of the lines that she had told her on so many occasions. Kimberly was a devout Christian but never tried to force the word down Chinirika's throat. Once she turned eighteen and moved out of her house but she would always try to be encouraging and subtly try to get her to change her ways for the better. Her mother's pleas fell on deaf ears and even while she walked behind Chop to what she was sure to be her death, the words just would not penetrate her heart.

~16~

"Then you will know the truth, and the truth will set you free."

John 8:32

"He lied to me all of these years," Haven said more to herself than to anyone else.

The news articles that she had read over and over again were shaking like leaves in an Autumn breeze. Tears clouded her eyes and her heart pounded rapidly. To know that the one man that you always loved unconditionally and trusted had lied to you your whole life was just something that Haven couldn't wrap her mind around.

Trouble didn't want to be the bearer of bad news but he knew that once he learned of the truth Haven deserved it just as much. He didn't want to be another man in her life that would knowingly and willingly continue to lie to her so he put it all out there. Granna had told her some things, like the plot that Chop had to kill her but it wasn't her place to tell her why. It also wasn't her place to tell Haven about Trouble's involvement in it but she did let her know that she needed to hear him out.

She explained how Chop wasn't one to go against and she was sure that Trouble was in a hard predicament.

When he'd pulled out the news articles that dated back to the Christmas Eve of 1999, Haven's heart shattered into dust. Her beautiful mother's face looked back at her and it was almost like Haven was looking into a mirror. Never once had she thought to ask any more questions about her mother once her father informed her of her death. There was no need too because she knew how aggressive cancer could be. He never let on that what he was saying wasn't the truth and she had believed him. Now there she was reading the details of how her mother lost her young life and it was a miracle that the baby that was in the room had survived.

"But why? How?" Haven asked no one in particular. She looked back and forth between Trouble and Granna waiting on someone to give her something that she could wrap her mind around.

Trouble sighed before he began his speel and he silently prayed that once he was done that he wouldn't lose Haven. He may not have been around her in the beginning for the right reasons but he certainly was then. It didn't take long for her to win his heart and now that she had it he didn't want her to let it go.

"First let me start off by telling you that I love you. You know that right?"

"Why do you sound like we're on an episode of Maury and you're about to tell me that you cheated or something?" Haven responded. Her mouth didn't form a smile but there was a hint of one in her eyes.

Trouble shook his head and had to admit that he did sound like that but he was glad that she wasn't looking too alarmed. Maybe she did trust that he wouldn't hurt her intentionally and whatever he was about to tell her wouldn't be so bad.

"Yes I know you love me and I love you too," she continued. Reaching over she put the news articles down and grabbed his hand with her own.

"I didn't know that when we first met that it was a setup. I just thought we were pulling up on some random girls because Fangas wanted to spit that weak game that he thought he had."

"Weak is an understatement with his lil' ugly self."

"I thought that he just wanted me to occupy your time while he got at Mila. It's not like it was uncommon for us to run game like that because we had done it before. The only thing was this time was different. As soon as I got out of the car and introduced myself, there was this thing about you. Like there was something special there. It didn't matter what I drove or what I was wearing. None of that appealed to you. The one thing that did stand out the most was my tattoo of the scripture.

You didn't turn your nose up at me when I explained my reason behind it but you embraced it. Man, I know I'm probably making no sense and just rambling," he told her.

Trouble swiped his free hand down the front of his face and blew out a deep breath. He had so many thoughts and emotions running through his mind that he didn't know if they were coming out right. Never in his life had he felt the need to explain himself to any other woman or girl besides his grandmother and there he was doing the opposite.

"It's ok Asa," Haven comforted him.

Asa. The way she said his name always gave him a sense of peace.

"After we left that day I got a call from my old man to tell me that he needed to meet with me. I wasn't up to dealing with him right then but I knew that if I didn't go I would pay for disobeying. That just wasn't something that I was willing to deal with right then."

Granna had explained to Haven already the type of man Chop was and that anyone who went against him would pay severely. She knew the moment that he showed up to her house to take Asa away on his thirteenth birthday that she had no say in the matter. If she did she wouldn't have lived long enough to see them pull out of the driveway. The last thing that she wanted was for her life to end before she could really make sure that Trouble could live in this world without her. She prayed day in and day out for him from the time she knew her daughter was pregnant with him up until the very moment he had just walked into her house. It was important for Haven to know the background of the type of person Chop was. That way she could understand the choices that Trouble made.

"The whole way to his meeting spot I couldn't stop thinking about the shy and insecure girl that I had just met. I kind of felt like I wanted to or had to protect you. I wasn't big on all things spiritual even though Granna was constantly trying to get me to be. It wasn't until meeting you that I started feeling differently. It happened so fast though.

Anyway, when I got to the meeting my old man slid a picture of you over to me and told me that he needed me to get close to you but he wouldn't tell me why. All he said was to get you to trust me and then I was supposed to bring you to him. I hesitated a minute but then I thought about the consequences I would face had I told him no. So I agreed. What I didn't know was that Fangas had more information than I knew at the time and he was planning things with Chop behind my back."

Haven sat there about to pass out because she was holding her breath and trying to make sense of everything she was being told. Trouble could tell that she was going through a mental battle but she deserved to know everything that he did.

"The night that we came over to your house changed everything for me though. Not just because we had sex but because of our conversation in your closet. I knew that you were the real deal and that night I understood why you were sent to me. It may have been a plan created by the enemy but it was only because God allowed it."

"I know that's right baby!" Granna said excitedly. She loved hearing her baby talking about God. It wasn't often but it was more than before.

"Were you going to kill me?" Haven asked.

"I honestly don't know."

Haven didn't know how to feel about hearing him tell her that. It wasn't his plan to harm her it was his father's but it still made her question things.

"How did you find out what was going on?" she asked.

"I overheard Fangas running his mouth one day and knew that I had to make a plan of my own. That's when I came to Granna and she helped me. We moved her out of her old house so that once I got you away you both would be safe. That's what I wanted to tell you the night of your prom but things went left too fast."

"What happens now? My daddy is going to jail for what I know will be the rest of his life. I don't have anyone else," Haven broke down crying.

Trouble pulled her close to him and let her cry all of her emotions out on his shoulder. Granna sat there watching them and felt sorry for the both of them. Neither should have had to deal with the things that they were facing at such a young age but in the end she knew they would be strong together. The silence was deafening until Granna thought of something.

"Baby let me see those articles for a minute."

Trouble handed them to her and refocused his attention on Haven. Granna put on her glasses and bit her bottom lip. Something that she did when she was always in deep thought.

"Hmmm interesting," she mumbled.

"What?" Trouble wanted to know.

"You brought me every article and clip that you could find right?"

"Yes ma'am."

"I don't see anything that mentions a funeral or funeral arrangements. Usually when anyone dies newspapers also run an obituary."

"What are you saying Granna?"

Haven sat quietly listening and wondered if Granna was saying what she thought. She quickly reached for the cell phone that sat on the table and went to the Safari browser. As soon as Google pulled up she typed in *Kenya Abrams obituary*. While the screen loaded Trouble looked over her shoulder and waited. If her mother didn't have an obituary then that only meant one thing and that was that she was still alive.

When there were no results that showed up Haven gasped. Not finding anything didn't necessarily mean that there wasn't one but what if that was exactly what it meant? Her mother being alive would change everything and cause even more questions to come about. If she was alive where was she and why didn't she come for her? More importantly, did she even want to have anything to do with her daughter?

"Something isn't right. Did you notice this?" Granna asked passing one of the articles back to Haven.

Haven didn't know why she wanted her to read over something that she had read more than once. She had combed those articles with a fine toothed comb looking for anything may have been missed but came up empty handed. There was nothing that stood out until it clicked. It wasn't about what was *on* the page but more about what was missing that changed everything!

~17~

"Do not be deceived: God will not be mocked. A man reaps what he sows."

Galatians 6:7

Chinirika wasn't the only one that was living a double life someone else was doing the same thing.

The sound of the door opening let Meech know that it was show time and he was ready to pull the final curtain. In walked Chop followed by Chinirika who looked like she was about to mess up her draws at any second.

"Have a seat," Chop ordered.

Nervously she did as she was told as a lone tear fell from her eyes. She already knew that it was the end of the road for her. Meech stood with the gun resting comfortably in his hand waiting on the go ahead.

"I'm not sure what kind of fool you take me for. You think I'm a fool?" Chop sat down in front of her and asked. His back was to Meech which was a big mistake on his part. Chop was so cocky and arrogant that he thought he was untouchable and no one would ever try him from behind.

"Of course I don't baby. You know that."

"Nah I don't know that. What I do know is that baby you're carrying in your gut isn't mine."

Chinirika didn't have to say a word to confirm what he had just said because her face told it all. How could he possibly know that she was pregnant and it wasn't his? She had been so careful. Even faced with the truth she still decided to try her luck and lie.

"I was going to tell you Shea! I knew that you didn't want any more kids but I was hoping that if I found the right way to tell you that you would accept it."

"You believe this broad?" Chop laughed and turned to Meech. He couldn't believe that she had to audacity to still sit in his face and lie.

"I'm telling truth. I know that you weren't able to raise Trouble so I figured that you would have another chance with this one. God is giving you another opportunity."

"God? God?! You mean that same God y'all was using to pimp the saints every time the doors to that church opened. Hilarious," Chop taunted.

"You know what? You're right! This is Keys' baby and he would be a better father than you could ever be. Just like he's a bigger boss than you and you couldn't handle it. That nigga stole all of your stuff, took a loss, set up shop once again from the bottom, and leveled up on that ass yet again. I see why you mad boo," Chinirika bragged. Fear had left her body and anger had taken over. If she was going to die she was going to make sure to crash Chop's face before she did and from the looks of it she had been successful.

Pow! Pow! Pow! Pow! Pow! Pow!

Chop emptied the gun inside of her body. Hearing her tell him all of the things that he had thought about over the years just sent him into a frenzy. Meech on the other hand was as cool as a cucumber.

"I didn't see that coming," Meech admitted. "I guess just like you didn't see this."

Turning around Chop's eyes got wide as he looked down the barrels of Meech's two guns. Confusion was evident but Meech didn't have a problem clearing up some things for him before he joined Chinirika.

"See the difference between you and Keys was that he was always about his money. You on the other hand focused more on getting back at him. But you did have something in common though," Meech explained.

"And what's that?" Chop asked smugly.

Chop stood there kicking himself for using all of his bullets on Chinirika and now he was in a position that he had never been in before. He was always the one that was on point and the one time he had been caught slipping it was about to cost him his life.

"Neither one of y'all paid attention to who you put on your team," he responded confusing Chop even more.

"I always know who's on my team," Chop told him.

"Did you know that you had Kenya's brother on your team?" Meech smirked.

"What?"

Pow!

"Arghhh!" Chop screamed out in pain as the bullet from Meech's gun entered his left knee. Falling to the floor in pain Chop wasn't as concerned about what his body was feeling but what his mind was thinking. Had he been that focused and dead set on getting back at Keys that he had in fact been caught slipping?

"Imagine your mother getting a phone call the night before Christmas and the police telling her that her only daughter had been shot. Do you know how that feels to see the woman that birthed you struggle to breathe after hearing that?" Meech asked as he remembered the night like it was the day before.

He had just stopped by his mother's house to drop off the gifts that he had gotten for her and the rest of his family. Although Janice had been upset with how his sister Kenya threw her life away for Keys, now that she had a granddaughter she wanted to make amends.

Janice had planned on having the whole family over in order to meet their newest family member but as soon as she answered that phone things changed. They rushed down to the hospital just to hear that Kenya didn't make it. Guilt immediately consumed Janice and she blamed herself for her daughter's death. Had she been supportive instead of cutting her child off then maybe she would have still been alive. Being a child of God and taking her faith seriously, Janice prayed for forgiveness for how she treated Kenya and hoped that she could at least make it up to her by having a good relationship with her granddaughter. Sadly, that wouldn't happen either. She had never even laid eyes on Haven and her heart was further crushed when she found out that an innocent baby had lost her life as well.

"My mama had to be admitted to the hospital herself because her heart almost gave out on her. It was only when the doctors rushed in to tell us that they were able to get Kenya back. What a mighty God we serve right?" Meech revealed. The way Chop's eyes grew as wide as saucers was comical to Meech.

"Kenya's alive?"

"I made a promise to my sister when I stood on the side of her hospital bed," Meech began ignoring Chop's question. It was no secret that he wanted Kenya and she had no interest in him. Meech had been almost five years older than his sister but she was his protector and confidant.

When everyone else turned their backs on her for her involvement with Keys, he was the one that stood by her. He didn't care too much for Keys either considering that he felt Kenya could do better and deserved better but he wasn't about to turn his back on his baby sister. Because of that he was privy to every area of not just her life but Keys as well.

"I told her that I would make sure my niece would be taken care of and before I took my last breath both you and Keys would have already taken yours."

"Speaking of my team, you must have forgotten about who I have on mine. If I don't show up after leaving here as planned Trouble and everyone else gonna be on your head. They already knew that I was meeting up with you," Chop said like he had just revealed something major causing Meech to laugh.

Pow!

"Arghhh!" Chop screamed out in agony again. The pain was excruciating and it felt like the both of his kneecaps were shattered by the bullets that had entered them.

Refusing to acknowledge what Chop had just said with words, Meech pulled out his cell phone and placed a call. The line trilled invading the space of the small front room that the two men sat in and on the third ring someone answered.

"Is it done yet?" Tonio asked with a voice full of excitement.

"Almost. Ya boy seems to think that y'all gonna come for my head if he doesn't show up after. You know considering the fact that everyone knew he was meeting up with me."

Tonio had been down with Chop since New York and things had always been good with them on the business side. That's why when he had been asked to set up shop down south it was a no brainer. He was down to make sure that his family continued to eat good but things changed. Tonio was big on loyalty and not switching up just for a dollar. Once he found out all of the things that Chop had done to him and the others that worked for him, all respect was lost. It took them all years to learn that Chop was only loyal to himself and that caused them to want no parts of him or the drug business anymore.

Chop sat on the floor next to Chinirika's lifeless body in shock to hear Tonio use so many expletives to describe him and how each one of his workers felt about their boss. To know that his ways had finally caught up to him just like Keys' should have been enough for him to beg for his life but it wasn't.

When Meech ended the call he just sat there watching Chop waiting for him to say something but he never did. Getting up from his seat he walked over to Chop with nothing but murder in his eyes.

"My mama's favorite scripture for as long as I can remember has always been Galatians six and seven. *Do not be deceived: God will not be mocked. A man reaps what he sows.* She said, 'Good or bad you will reap a harvest of whatever it was that you planted'," Meech recited.

"Man go ahead and kill me. Don't nobody want to hear no sermon. You about to commit a sin but want to get all holy on me now," Chop seethed.

"As you wish."

Meech let off the rest of his rounds into Chop before walking out of the front door ending the reign of terror that had been going on for years. The sins that both he and Chop had committed may have varied but when it came down to how bad they stunk in the nostrils of God, they all smelled the same.

Unlike Chop and Keys, Meech would do anything to protect his family and loved them unconditionally. True enough, the countless lives he had taken and the many streets he had flooded with drugs for that mighty dollar made him no better. One day he would have to pay for everything he had done as well. Until then he would just light up the blunt that he had in the ashtray just like the flames of the house burning in his rearview mirror.

~18~

"Then I will give you shepherds after my own heart who will lead you with knowledge and understanding."

Jeremiah 3:15

Keys sat out in the yard looking at the inmates that surrounded him. For years to come that would be his home and those would be his roommates. Considering he had yet to get a court date he didn't know exactly how long he would be there but he was prepared for a long sentence.

What bothered him even more was that he had got caught slipping in the worst way, by not just the FEDS but his number one enemy. Never in a million years would he have thought that Chop would find him. Everything he had done had been calculated just so that wouldn't happen. It wasn't that he was scared of anything because Keys feared no one, not even God. He just didn't want all of his secrets to be found out. Just when he thought he was untouchable he was touched.

Overnight he had gone from what people thought was prominent leader in a church to just another black man behind bars. That was exactly what the detective on the case had called him on the day he was arrested and his empire had fallen.

"I'm Detective Collins," the tall dark skin man announced walking into the interrogation room.

Keys had been in that small room for almost five hours before someone came in to talk to him. By the looks of the detective that was now sitting across from him, he wasn't one to be played with.

"I'm so disgusted by these charges that I won't even beat around the bush. You're going down and if I have anything to do with it, it will be for a long time."

"Whatever man," Keys blew him off. He didn't want to hear something that he already knew.

"I've seen people get arrested for almost everything under the sun so the drugs and murders don't surprise me. What does surprise me is that you had the audacity to play with God by claiming to be a servant of His. You give good pastors who are really about this life a bad name."

"I don't know what you're talking about. None of that stuff you found belongs to me and I don't know how it got in there. As a man of the cloth I would never disrespect God like this," Keys lied.

"Wowwww. Unbelievable," Detective Collins scoffed. "I stand in front of my congregation every Sunday and Wednesday doing my best to lead God's people back to Him and pray that I don't do anything to cause them to fall while under my leadership. I'm responsible for those souls that I'm teaching. Do you understand that their blood is on my hand if I lead them astray?"

"Whatever man. Those people grown and gonna do what they want to no matter what I say."

Keys couldn't lie and say that he knew exactly what Detective Collins meant. He only picked out scriptures that he knew would cause the people in his church to cough up the big bucks and make him look like he knew what he was doing. Initially he didn't start the church to preach he just wanted to look the part. When people started coming in he had to actually get up there and do something. Keys figured since he didn't study the word enough to know what he was preaching eventually someone would call him out on it. When they didn't, he knew that he could pull the wool over their eyes. He was the epitome of a wolf in sheep's clothing and loved every minute of it. Not only was he was making money from their tithes but he was able to push more dope than he ever had. Work was being moved undetected and that was all the motivation he needed to keep going.

Shaking his head Detective Collins sat there stunned at how nonchalant Keys was acting. To know that he felt absolutely nothing about what he had done began to make him angry.

"They may be grown but what about your daughter?" he asked.

Instantly Keys felt like he had been hit with a ton of bricks at the mention of Haven. She was still missing and he hadn't thought of her not once since he had gotten arrested. His main concern was trying to make sure that he got out of there and how he was going to recoup all of the money he had lost.

After another thirty minutes passed by before the detective finally gave up and officially charged him with everything under the sun. Keys had been waiting for a court date ever since, six months to be exact. Sleepless night after sleepless night he tossed and turned trying to think of a plan. Every number that he had stored in his memory bank he had used and each call went unanswered. Giving up on trying to think of a plan for the time being, Keys exited the yard and headed back to his cell. All he wanted to do was catch a quick nap to let his mind recharge so that he could think clearly.

***

A few hours later Keys was being awakened to the sound of the guard calling his name to inform him that he had a visitor. The only person that he could think of that would be there to see him would be his lawyer since everyone else had turned their backs on him. Hopefully this visit would be to tell him that he had a court date and not that there were more charges.

Keys walked down the corridor until the guard stopped him at the visiting room door. His head was down when he entered and it wasn't until he looked up to see Haven sitting there that guilt slapped him in the face.

"Baby girl! Are you alright? Where have you been? God knows I was worried about you," he told her rushing over to where she sat. He stopped abruptly when he saw the look on his daughter's face.

"Were you worried about me when you lied to me about Mama?" she asked getting right to the point.

Keys felt like his legs were going to give out on him at the mention of Kenya. That was a secret that he had hoped to take to his grave right along with the other things he had done. For years he never worried about the truth coming out since Kenya was dead. Her side of the family disowned her once she chose him over them. The one time she did try to go around was to let them know that she was pregnant. She was full of hope that would change their minds, it only made things worse.

"Haven listen to me. I did what was best for you at the time," he tried convincing her.

"The best for me? The best for me would be for my father not to lie to me! The best for me would have been for my father to open his eyes and realize that I was more important than the streets. I could have died right along with Mama but for whatever reason God spared me. Doesn't that count for anything?"

Tears began to flow down her face and Keys wanted to be there for her but he knew that it was too late. The damage was already done and he didn't know if anything could be repaired. The least that he could do was be honest with her at that moment. Taking a deep breath, he finally opened up.

"You're right baby. I was selfish and consumed with becoming the biggest kingpin to ever do it. Your mother was really the love of my life no matter what you may believe. She was just caught up in my web and paid the ultimate price for that. If it wasn't for me robbing one of my rivals Ken may still be alive. I'm sorry baby for all of this."

Shaking her head, Haven couldn't believe what she was hearing from the man she had looked to as her protector. He went on to explain everything to her no matter how hard it was to be reminded of the things that he had done. Her lungs searched for oxygen and she could feel herself going into a panic attack. Some of the things that Keys was telling her was just too much to hear and there was still one last thing that she needed an answer to. Unfortunately, she wouldn't receive it that day.

"Baby you alright?" Keys asked nervously.

Even if Haven wanted to reply she couldn't. The only thing that she could do was shake her head no.

"Aye! Guard! Somebody!" Keys yelled as he rushed over to her. "Hold on baby. Daddy's right here."

"My…my…" Haven tried to speak but the pain she was now feeling was making everything worse.

"Back up!" one of the guards along with the nurse told Keys. Although he didn't want to leave his daughter's side he knew that it was best so that she could get help.

Not too long after, the EMTs arrived and placed her on a stretcher with oxygen. Keys was so focused on her face that he didn't realize what was going on in front of him until someone got his attention.

"What's her name?" the young lady asked.

"Haven," Keys replied.

"Haven can you hear me?"

Nodding her head Haven confirmed that she could.

"How far along are you?"

"What?!" Keys yelled. His eyes traveled from Haven's tear stained face down to where her hands were resting on the small but noticeable baby bump.

"I'm sorry Daddy," was the last thing that Keys heard as he stood by and watched the medics rush her out of the building.

His baby was having a baby.

~19~

"I waited patiently for the Lord; He turned to me and heard my cry."

Psalm 40:1

Day in and day out Haven found herself going through a plethora of emotions. One minute she was extremely happy and the next she was crying her pretty eyes out. No matter how she felt though she was thankful to have Trouble and Granna by her side. With her father in jail and facing life there was no one else that she could stay with so he had no choice but to agree to her moving in with Granna. It just so happened that Trouble was in the same boat as she was. Once it was confirmed that his father had been found dead in a burned down house he too was right back where he should have been in the first place.

Granna was glad to have them both with her. She hated being alone at times and now she had company. Besides she had grown to love Haven just as much, if not more than her grandbaby. Haven reminded her so much of her own daughter and she understood why Asa had fallen so hard for her. That girl was as genuine as they came but no matter how Granna felt she had rules in place. They could be together all day long but when it was time to go to bed they knew to sleep in separate rooms. A baby may have been on the way but they better not even think about going down that road again unless they were married. Haven thought that she was going to burst her water from laughing when Granna told them they better throw those thoughts into the sea of forgetfulness. That old woman was a mess but Haven loved her.

"Here come Little Miss Fastness," Granna said looking out of the window. She didn't miss a beat when it came to what was going on outside of that window of hers. Haven often said that Granna reminded her of Pearl from that old show *227*. For her to stay to herself she sure did know everything.

"Granna leave my bestie alone," Haven laughed. Before she had the chance to get up and go to the door Trouble entered from the kitchen.

"Rest. I got it bae," he told Haven causing her cheeks to hurt from the smile that spread across her face.

"Hey bro!" Mila greeted before giving Trouble hug.

The night of their prom Mila thought she was going to lose it when she couldn't find Haven. If there had ever been anyone that Mila would have given her life for it was that girl. Bullets were flying but that didn't matter. All she cared about was making sure that her best friend was safe and if she died to protect her it was worth it. That was just the bond that they had.

For days Mila cried and prayed more than she ever had in her life. It was that incident that made her realize that God was trying to get her attention. Her ways had been all wrong and she needed to make a change. When the news announced that their classmate Krista had been found dead it hit Mila that that could have very well been her or Haven but it wasn't. She had been given another opportunity to get herself together and she wasn't going to take that for granted.

Trouble knew how close the girls were but he was also aware of the fact that he was being followed. He had wanted to tell Mila right away that Haven was safe but he couldn't risk someone finding out where she lived and hurting her. That would crush Haven and she didn't need any more pain invading her life. Trouble believed he was sent to protect her and that was what he was going to do.

It took some planning but he was able to get a message to Mila that her girl was good but even then that wasn't enough. If she couldn't see her right away she at least wanted to hear her voice. Just like he's promised Trouble made it happen. Once she was convinced Mila was able to wait patiently until they could be reunited again.

"Hey sis," Trouble responded.

"Hey Granna!" Mila said excitedly.

"Hey little fastness. Come give me my hug." Granna talked about Mila but it was all in fun. She loved her as well and was glad that God had given her a wakeup call too.

"Look at TeeTee's baby!" Mila squealed rushing over to rub on Haven's rotund belly. She couldn't wait until her niece entered the world to be spoiled.

"Stop nut! Every time you do that it takes hours for her to settle back down," Haven laughed.

"Well hurry up and spit her out then so I can spoil my baby. Oh, here before I forget," Mila announced before going into her bag and pulling out two envelopes. She passed one to Haven and the other to Trouble.

Opening the envelope tears began to form in Haven's eyes as she looked at her high school diploma. After everything that happened months ago there was no way that she could return to school but thankfully she had taken school serious for twelve years. Because of that she had more than enough credits to graduate on time and with honors.

"That's my girl!" Granna said happily.

"I hate that I wasn't able to see you walk across that stage sis," Haven told her sadly.

"I know we always said we would walk it together. That's why I didn't walk," she announced.

"What?"

"Girl why you yellin'? You know good and well I was not about to walk without my sister with me. So this just means that when we graduate college you better not be full of another baby. We gone twerk all across the stage!"

The three of them shared a laugh until Haven noticed Trouble standing there still holding the unopened envelope.

"Asa?"

It took her a minute to get up off the couch but once she did she made her way over to him. Granna and Mila sat silently waiting to find out the reason he had such a faraway look in his eyes. He was so deep into his thoughts that he didn't realize that Haven was in his space until she touched him.

"What's wrong?" she asked him.

Following his eyes, hers landed on the envelope that he held.

"You open it," was all he said. Trouble didn't think that he would be as nervous as he was. Knowing that the results of his GED test had finally arrived had him shaking.

When Chop pulled him out of school and placed him on the streets, Trouble hadn't even had the chance to start high school. Being around Haven and having his mind renewed made him want to go back. It wasn't a high school diploma but at least he could use it in order to further his education. Trouble knew that if he wanted to stand up and be the man that Haven and his daughter needed, he had to have something under his belt. The dope money wasn't anything he wanted to continue to use. There was too much blood that was shed for those dollars.

Haven was there every step of the way. She helped him study and was patient with him when he was frustrated with himself. Never once did Trouble feel like she looked down on him. Instead she helped to lift him up.

While Haven was opening the envelope, everyone held their breath. She read over the contents with an expression that no one could read.

"What does it say?" Granna asked impatiently.

"Um.."

"Girrrl I know you better spill that tea," Mila sassed.

"Congratulations baby you did it!"

"Huh?" Trouble asked in shock.

"You passed all four sections with flying colors. Look."

Trouble took the paper out of her hand and read over it himself. He couldn't believe it was real. A lot of the stuff he struggled with during the practice test, so to see that he aced it had him at a loss for words.

"Glory be to God!" Granna yelled. She couldn't stop the tears even if she wanted to. Nothing in this world could have made her any prouder of him than she was right then.

"I'm so proud of you Asa. You worked hard and it paid off," Haven beamed.

"I couldn't have done it without you. Thank you for not making me feel dumb or less than. You have no idea how the encouragement that you and Granna gave me helped," he replied honestly.

"That's because I believe in you and I know that God has greater in store for you."

"I know. That's why instead of me going to college for something else I've decided to go to seminary school."

"Heyyyy glorayyyyy!" Granna shouted.

Trouble thought long and hard about what it was that he wanted to do with his life. After everything he had witnessed and the many talks he had with God, he knew that he had to answer the call. There was no way that Trouble had gone through everything that he had for nothing. He was to use those situations to help others. Unlike Keys, Trouble was going to do right by the people of God. Every message he delivered would be straight from the mouth of God Himself.

After celebrating the success of both Trouble and Haven with dinner, everyone decided to call it a night. Mila chose to stay the night and go home the next day. She wanted to let her girl in on her new love interest but before they could get comfortable to chat, little Miss Kenya Atlantis Thomas wanted to make her debut.

"Asaaaa! Grannaaaa!" Haven screamed. It sounded like a heard of elephants stampeding through the house as they ran to her.

"What's wrong?" the two of them answered at the same time. For Granna to be old she sure could move fast.

"Owww!"

"Her water just broke and we need to go," Mila informed them.

It took less than twenty minutes to get to the hospital. The whole way there, Haven cried out in pain while Mila did her best to calm her down. Granna spent the whole time praying while Trouble drove like a bat out of hell. By the time the nurses had gotten Haven checked in, her doctor had arrived and she was ready to push.

The piercing screams that filled the air after the last push were like music to their ears. Kenya was the perfect mix of both Trouble and Haven. She had a head full of thick curly hair that was already long enough to put in a ponytail. Her skin looked like smooth butterscotch covered in freckles like her mother. While her golden eyes came straight from her father. Their baby was perfect.

"I can't wait to dress her up," Mila gushed.

"Mi she is not a baby doll," Trouble told her.

"But she's gonna be so flyyy," Mila whined.

Haven watched as her family doted over her daughter and her heart was torn. She was happy that her daughter was healthy and she had the love of the people standing in the room. Then there was the part of her heart that ached. Neither Keys or Kenya were there to witness the birth of their first grandchild.

Before she got so deep in to her thoughts there was a knock at the door.

"Come in," Haven called out and when the door opened her world stopped.

"Mama?"

~Epilogue~

"And now, God of Israel, let your word that you promised your servant David, my father, come true."

1 Kings 8:26

Pastor Asa Thomas sat behind the pulpit as the praise team ministered in song. It was his first official service as the lead pastor in their new church. People of all ages and races sat waiting on him to deliver a word from God that they could apply to their lives. If someone had told him seven years prior that he would be standing where he was, he would have laughed in their faces. But there he was doing just that and enjoying every minute of it.

Looking out into the congregation, his eyes landed on his beautiful First Lady as she smiled. Haven had grown into an even more beautiful woman than she was when he first met her. While he studied ministry in college, Haven decided to become a social worker. The heart that she was blessed with made her want to be there for others. So many times, there were kids that had been mistreated and she wanted to change that. Haven knew that sadly the system didn't always have children's best interest at heart. Her husband's young life was indicative of just that. When he was taken out of school never to return, no one thought enough to check on his wellbeing. They probably looked at him as just another rebellious black boy that was going to get himself killed in the streets. That would be one less thug they would have to worry about.

While he watched her, Haven watched him. Admiration was evident in her eyes. Trouble the boy had transformed into Asa the man. A man that loved God and his family above all else. The one that allowed God to use him for His glory and to be a provider. Each day Haven thanked God for sending him to her. No matter the circumstances that brought them together it worked out for the good of them both.

Haven sometimes thought about how she could have turned away from Asa once she knew the truth but she didn't. It wasn't his fault that he was placed in that situation so she would never hold it against him.

"I knew when I first met him that he loved my baby."

"And God knows I love me some him," Haven replied.

Haven turned to her right and looked at her mother. Never in a million years did she think the opportunity would ever present itself. For as long as she could remember, all Haven thought about was what it would be like to just sit in her presence.

The day they were at Granna's house and Asa showed up changed everything. The last article that Haven read revealed something that she hadn't noticed at first. Not only did it speak on the death of her mother but hers as well. The first time Haven went to speak with her father in jail she gave him the opportunity to get everything out. Before she could get the most important question answered she was rushed off to the hospital. It wasn't until almost a month later that she was able to go back. Keys knew that he could no longer sit on that information since the truth was out. Finally growing tired he told her what she needed to know.

Keys explained that when he came home to find Kenya shot he thought Haven was dead as well. There was blood everywhere. When she cried out, immediately Keys knew that he had to protect her. He failed when it came to protecting Kenya and he wasn't willing to do it again. It was common knowledge that being in the streets you needed a few dirty cops on payroll. Because of this, it was only a matter of time before Chop found out that Haven was still alive and come for her.

Police weren't trustworthy in Keys' eyes but there were a few that he could trust. One in particular, his uncle Jeffery, had been in law enforcement for almost thirty years. He had some connections and was able to come up with a plan. They would report that everyone in the apartment during the shooting had perished. Even a two week old baby. In reality Haven was just fine. Keys left New York immediately after giving his statement so he had no idea that Kenya pulled through. Keys may have been in the dark about Haven's mother but Meech wasn't.

For six months Kenya lay in a hospital bed under an alias until she came to. When she did her family, just like Keys, got out of dodge. If it wasn't for Kenya's bother Meech, no one would have known Haven was alive. Although Meech knew, it was years before he never told anyone else. There was the real possibility that Kenya and Haven would be upset about him keeping that secret but he couldn't risk their safety.

There had always been a bond between Asa and Meech but it only got stronger once Haven came into the picture. It was Meech that Asa had confided in when he wanted to go against his own father for her. The two of them together came up with how they would protect her. When Keys was arrested and Chop was killed, Meech was finally able to let the secret out.

Just as he had predicted Kenya was upset she didn't know sooner her daughter was alive. Once she heard him out she understood where Meech was coming from and was thankful that he had kept a close eye on Haven. As long as she wasn't mistreated then that was the most important thing to Kenya.

Haven had gone into labor before they had a chance to let her know about her mother. Her pregnancy ended up being a high risk one due to the severe hypertension she had been diagnosed with. The last thing anyone wanted was for the news of Kenya being alive to cause any harm to the baby or Haven so they waited. When Haven looked up and saw the woman she had yearned for walk into her hospital room she broke down. Years of tears rushed down her face and the sobs that escaped her mouth made her whole body shake. Kenya held onto Haven as if her life depended on it as they cried together.

The reunion may have been long overdue but each day they made up for the time lost. Kenya was there to help raise her only granddaughter, watch Haven walk down the aisle on her wedding day, and couldn't wait to be in the delivery room when her grandson arrived in a couple of weeks. Every day Kenya thanked God for sparing her life. She may have had to use a tracheostomy tube for the rest of her life but she didn't care. As long as she could be present in Haven's life nothing else mattered.

Haven looked around at the new faces as well as some of the old. It surprised her that quite a few members that were a part of the church when her father was there had returned. He had caused so much damage resulting in some of them to fall away from God.

Twice a month Haven made the trip to visit her father. He had been sentenced to two consecutive life sentences and would never see the light of day again. Although she was upset about the things he had done, that was still her father. She loved him and that would never change. Hosea no longer went by the name Keys and had finally allowed God to renew his mind. He had so much time to think about how he'd hurt so many and realized a change needed to take place. Getting saved for real was his first step. People may not have believed he was capable of changing but for once Hosea didn't do it for anyone else. No longer would he use and abuse the grace and mercy that was given to him.

Still in shock after Haven told him about Kenya, it took him a while to want to see her. He had done so much wrong and he was ashamed to face her. During one visit, Haven told him to that the opportunity to apologize and ask her mother for forgiveness. Surprisingly, Kenya did. She too had been given another chance and was going to make the best of it. On the weekends that Haven didn't go to visit, Kenya was there. Not to rekindle any romantic relationship but to salvage the friendship they once had.

"As I stand before you this morning, I understand the great task that I have in front of me. A task that I don't take lightly. Some days I ask God why me? And each time I get the same answer. Why not you? I won't get up here and act like I have it altogether because I don't. I fall daily and have moments where I second guess myself. Notice that I said myself. Because God is so mighty and so awesome there is no way that I can or will ever second guess Him.

I don't have all of the answers or know everything there is to know about this walk with Christ. The one thing that I do know is, I will fear no evil; for thou art with me."

The End

Author's Note

To God be the glory for another book! This ride has been amazing and I'm so thankful that He is continuing to use me this way. I've written more books than I ever imagined I would and now it's time to branch out into another area. I will never stop writing but it will be in a different capacity. Don't get it twisted though, when it's time for me to write another book please believe I will!

For now, it's time for my name to be on the big screen...I'll see yall on the red carpet at my first movie premiere! Muah!

Made in the USA
Middletown, DE
03 June 2018